Morse Code for Romantics

to Alex

Morse Code

••• ——— •••

FOR ROMANTICS

ANNE BALDO

The Porcupine's Quill

Library and Archives Canada Cataloguing in Publication

Title: Morse code for romantics / Anne Baldo.

Names: Baldo, Anne, author.

Description: Short stories.

Identifiers: Canadiana (print) 20220477876 | Canadiana (ebook) 20220478058

   | ISBN 9780889844568 (softcover) | ISBN 9780889844575 (PDF)

Classification: LCC PS8603.A5285 M67 2022 | DDC C813/.6|–dc23

1   2   3   •   24   23   22

Published by The Porcupine's Quill, 68 Main Street, PO Box 160,

Erin, Ontario N0B 1T0. http://porcupinesquill.ca

Edited by Stephanie Small. Represented in Canada by Canadian Manda. Trade orders are available from University of Toronto Press.

We acknowledge the support of the Ontario Arts Council and the Canada Council for the Arts for our publishing program. The financial support of the Government of Canada is also gratefully acknowledged.

Canada Council for the Arts / Conseil des arts du Canada

ONTARIO ARTS COUNCIL
CONSEIL DES ARTS DE L'ONTARIO
an Ontario government agency
un organisme du gouvernement de l'Ontario

Canadä

Ontario
Ontario Media Development
Corporation

For my mother Rose, and my father Phillip,
with gratitude,

and for Jesse, with love.

TABLE OF CONTENTS

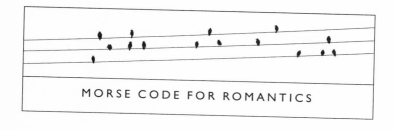

MORSE CODE FOR ROMANTICS

We are dressed to match the décor: pink peonies, floating in glass bowls of water and gold glitter. So our dresses are gold, too, with tulle skirts that swish the floor and bodices scaled with sequins. We look like mermaids, aquatic auguries of shipwrecks and drowning, or, depending on the folklore you consult, the souls of suicides dead before their weddings. Either way, we are hazardous girls, ready to wreck you on the coral reef of our teeth, tangle you with the cold kelp of our hair. We walk like mermaids too, suddenly rocked by the hard sensation of land, the heaviness of air. Except for us it isn't sea legs—it's only champagne.

We linger by the wedding cake, trying to delay going back to the head table, where we sit separated by the groom's younger brother, Heath. Hannah, the maid of honour, is stranded on the other side by Adam, the best man, another brother. 'I can't go back,' Hannah says.

'You have to. You're her sister.'

Across the hall, lit by strings of gold lights, Livvy sits at the head table in her wedding dress, chosen from what the woman at the bridal store had called the romance collection. Livvy had bought the first dress she tried on. *When you know, you just know,* the woman at the shop had said, beaming. *Like when you fall in love.*

Do you think that's really true? Livvy had asked, gazing at a display of pearl hair combs and crystal teardrop earrings, and the woman said, *Of course!* Smiling still but only with her lips.

Ivory lace over the shoulders. A bouquet of peonies and eucalyptus, stems wrapped in gold ribbon. It had taken three of us to tie the corset back of Livvy's dress—incorrectly, according to the photographer, who had sighed, retied it herself. I try to divine the look on Livvy's face, but she only sits there, removing peony petals from her bouquet one by one, stripping the stems clean.

Hannah says, 'I can't go back there and sit with Adam anymore. He just has these *theories* on everything. He's like, "You know the problem women have?"'

'Besides him, you mean?' I say absently as I watch Trevor, the new groom, lean away from Livvy to see something his friend Loreto shows him on the screen of his phone. Third period of the hockey game.

'Yeah. He says, "They're not real, anymore, women. They just pretend to be who you want them to be."'

'He wishes.'

We're quiet for a moment. Next to us, the white cake is speckled with gold, surrounded by pale macarons shaped like seashells on a beach. It looks like the layers are sprinkled with pearls, but they aren't real, of course. They're only sugar pearls. Adam would probably have a theory about this cake, how it pretends, too.

'I don't want to go back,' I say finally, 'but we have to, for Livvy. We're the bridesmaids.'

'What about Mila? She's a bridesmaid, too. Can't she go?'

'Mila's outside. Come on, we can't leave Livvy there alone.'

'A married woman's never alone,' Hannah says. 'She has her husband.'

At the bridal salon, months earlier, I had drifted through the sheaves of pale chiffon to find stacks of magazines arranged on glass tables. They were full of brides getting married in rustic barns, in vineyards. The palettes this season were supposed to be soft, the magazines said, sweet, blush and cream, shades that whispered.

I don't like the back, Livvy had said, *the corset.*

Of course, said the saleswoman, *you could always order the dress with buttons, instead,* and Trevor's mother said, *No, it has to be adjustable. She won't know how much room she needs until then.*

Oh, the woman had said. *I see.*

Hannah sighs. 'I'm going to steal a macaron, you want one?'

'No, thanks,' I say, 'I don't like meringue.' And anyway, I'm not hungry at all.

At the table, I slide into my chair next to Heath again, trying not to trip over my own skirt. He moves a knife around his plate morosely.

'What's wrong?'

'I can't eat meat on the bone,' he says, draping his linen napkin over the chicken. 'It reminds me too much of what it was.'

'You just want an anonymous blob?'

He cringes. 'Don't say it like that, either.'

'Maybe you need to become a vegetarian.'

'Maybe.' His dark hair has the raw, chopped look of a fresh haircut. The boutonnière pinned to his lapel, a pink peony, wilts slightly. 'I didn't know you were friends with Livvy.'

'I'm not, really. I was pressed into service, sort of.'

'Like the British Navy used to do.'

'Yes,' I say. 'But for the sake of symmetry, not the Age of Sail. Your mother really wanted an even number for the wedding party.'

I watch Livvy whisper something to Mila, finally back. Mila pulls Livvy to her feet, and they disappear into the crowd on the dance floor.

Livvy is older than Hannah and me, just by a year. I used to live for the days she'd cross the blacktop to visit us at recess on the junior side, where we sat in the shade with our sticker albums, peeling stickers off and trading them. Bright dinosaurs on skateboards, Mylar unicorns, *I love you* in shiny foil letters. Sandylion stickers from the Buck or Two at Tecumseh Mall. We bought all our treasures there: greasy lotion that smelled like coconut, plastic heart-shaped rings, green mood lipstick that changed to pink when we were happy. And Livvy—in grade eight she wore high heels to school on picture day, with black lace gloves, dark lipstick, a velvet choker. In the gym, as we lined up to be photographed, I caught her teacher exchanging a look of disapproval with another teacher, lips pursed in prim reprimand. Still, they always chose her to bring envelopes to the office, to award the student of the month. You could always count on her. Perfect attendance. She won the science fair three years in a row. Making plastic out of milk, growing crystals in an eggshell, breeding woolly blooms of mould in Petri dishes. I remembered her ribbons: blue for first place.

See you tomorrow at our shotgun wedding, Trevor had said in the parking lot of Franco's last night, as we all left the rehearsal dinner.

Livvy said, *No one's got a gun to your head.*

Adam rolled his eyes. *Relax already. It's a joke. Take it easy with the mood swings.*

I look past Heath, but Livvy is gone. Only the petals mark her place at the table, like the ones Persephone left behind in the field the moment she vanished.

'Should we say a toast?' The light from the votive candles licks Heath's fingers as he offers me a glass. Like his brothers he wears square gold cufflinks, a black silk tie with a slim gold clip. I let the lip of my glass ring against his.

At the bridal salon, Livvy had stood before the mirror, back in her own things. A heather-grey men's shirt, square hemline, pointed collar. She opened up the buttons, eyed the snug tugging of her camisole over her stomach. *Don't worry,* the woman said. *You'll get your body back in no time.* Livvy had lifted her face, looked up. *Where did it go?*

'I better go check on Livvy.'

There are children everywhere, screaming and running past the adults. I make my way through the crowd, through the doors, past the guestbook I still haven't signed, with the bride and groom's names blooming in raised gold foil along the spine. *Olivia & Trevor,* even though Livvy never uses her full name. I find her in the hall's washroom, through the screen of green silk ferns that border the doorway. There is a fainting couch off to the side, upholstered in deep burgundy, and she's there, her eyes closed, her eyelids shimmering with champagne powder.

It's too bad about Livvy, my mother had said as we knelt in the dirt planting switchgrass in the rain garden I was trying to make at the side of the house. Sometimes I looked around and felt overwhelmed by the city's grey asphalt, by parking lot after parking lot, by each cold spread of concrete, and I hoped this was the antidote. *She had so much potential.*

She still has potential now. I dropped a handful of mulch.

No, she had said, *it's not the same. Mothers don't have any use for potential, whether or not they ever had it. They become too busy nurturing it in others.*

'Livvy?'

'Hey, Jordan.' She wears a thin gold lariat around her neck, gold drop earrings. The makeup girl has overdone her, streaked her cheekbones with highlighter in two bronze slashes. 'Are you having a good time?'

'Yes,' I say, wondering if I should sit down beside her. Instead I stay where I stand, twisting the bracelet she'd given the bridesmaids, rose quartz and gold, around my wrist. 'You look beautiful.'

'Thank you. So do you.'

'You can't tell,' I say, and then blush, swarmed with regret. 'I mean, I shouldn't have said that—'

'No,' Livvy says. 'That's good. It will make his mom happy.'

I think of Livvy not in this white dress. In the clothes I know her in. Blue flannel and old jeans. Or getting ready to go out for the night, in what she called a black cami dress that looked like a slip. Double-strap Mary Jane heels and red lipstick gleaming like the last lick of jam in the jar. Standing in the doorway of Hannah's bedroom saying, *I'm going to lie down. When Trevor comes over just send him to my room,* while we slouched on Hannah's bed reading teen magazines with headlines like 'How I Got Him to Notice Me' and 'What's the Right Way to Kiss?' and 'Does He Like Me?' And Livvy would say, *Don't read that shit,* tossing us a copy of *The Bell Jar* before she left. I thought of Livvy last autumn, driving Hannah and me downtown to the Loop on Halloween. She was dressed for a party, bride of Dracula—thrift-store lace, lips bloodied, singing along with the song on the radio, her and Karen O begging you to wait.

Outside, the music slows down. 'Get ready, get ready,' the DJ says. 'We're just about to have the bouquet toss.'

Livvy gets to her feet. 'Shit, I lost my flowers.'

'You can have mine,' I say, offering her my peonies.

'Thanks, Jordan. You coming? I'll throw it to you.'

'I don't want to get married.'

'Good.'

She sighs, tries blending in the makeup on her cheeks, two bronze lacerations, with a crushed-up napkin. Closer I can smell the eucalyptus from her lost bouquet, and the perfume she always wears, J'adore.

'Are you all right?'

'Sure,' she says, and smiles. 'It could be worse.'

'Yeah.'

'I could be marrying Adam,' she says, adding, 'Can you imagine?' at the very same time I say it. We laugh. I try not to see it as a sign.

She leaves and I pretend I have to use the washroom, sit in a stall while the DJ tries to work up the crowd. 'Get ready, here we go,' he cries. 'The moment of truth. Good luck, girls.'

When I re-enter the hall, the bouquet toss is over. A pair of flower girls in tea-length dresses, white skirts brindled with gold, fight over it. Loose pink petals are strewn across the dance floor.

A few feet away, I see her, Livvy, swaying in Trevor's arms, her cheek on his shoulder, the black fabric of his suit (tailored, narrow lapel, Italian wool) sparkling gold from her makeup. 'Can't Help Falling in Love', their song, Elvis pleading for his love to take his hand, his whole life.

'Jordan?' It's Heath. 'Did you want to go for a walk?'

'Yeah, I do.'

In the entranceway we pass the gilt-framed portrait of Giuseppe Verdi, an opera composer, the hall's namesake. We pass the oil paintings of Italian landscapes. We keep walking through the smokers by the front doors, through the parking lot, to the edge of a scrubby field, dry green mixed with the wild starry blue of chicory.

Heath says, 'We were out one night, downtown at a bar, like a year ago, and Livvy took me by the hand and pushed me into the wall.'

'Really.'

'She said, "All right, Heath, show me."'

I try to breathe easy. 'What did she want you to show her?'

'She wanted me to kiss her,' he says. 'But I couldn't. Not somewhere like that.'

He doesn't look like his brothers. Not like Trevor, who is handsome in the fine, clean way of American football players from the 1950s—hard jaw, sturdy shoulders—or Adam, with the oily good looks of a billboard lawyer. Heath has the uneasy beauty of a Romantic poet—pale, consumptive maybe, lovelorn, the peak of high cheekbones, the hollow dip below.

The stars shimmer like smashed glass over us. For a moment we sit quietly enough that you can hear the sound of the freighters down on the Detroit River. Then he shrugs off his suit jacket, unbuttons his shirt to show me something over his collarbone, just below his shoulder.

'I got a tattoo.'

A sequence of black dots and dashes. 'Of what?'

'It's her name,' he said, fixing his shirt. 'In Morse code.'

'That doesn't seem like a good idea. What if your brother sees it?'

'He won't.'

'What if you wear a V-neck?'

'They don't look good on me.'

'Well, what if you go to the beach someday?'

He says, 'No one knows Morse code.'

'Some people do.'

'Who?'

'Lighthouse keepers,' I say. 'Girl detectives.'

Heath laughs. I reach over to push back his shirt a bit, see her name again. It is beautiful.

He says, 'Maybe I don't know how to show my love the right way.'

'Show me,' I say, 'what you would have shown her.'

We lie down in the field, a blue crush of chicory. *Grit your teeth*, they used to say, *grin and bear it*, back when grief was supposed to be good for you, when it could be turned into something useful, like how oysters turned pain into pearls. I think of her name tattooed on his shoulder, of lighthouses beaming out messages into the darkness of the night. *Livvy, Livvy, Livvy*. Of Morse code transmissions, little electric jumps sent out over a wire. But the beauty of Morse code is you could make a message of anything—car headlights, a horn, knots on a rope. The dotted light of stars blinking in constellations.

Heath tells me the universe is infinite. That there are other worlds like ours out there, other versions of us.

'I just tell myself that somewhere in space, I'm with her.'

'Does that work?' I ask.

And he says it does, sometimes. And maybe it is true. Maybe we would find each other one day, too, somewhere in the clouds, in a sky without stars.

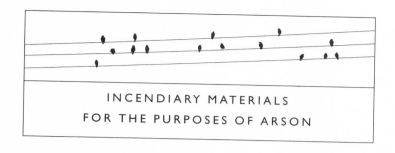

INCENDIARY MATERIALS
FOR THE PURPOSES OF ARSON

When Franco sees the front page of the paper he thinks, *Of course. Jules* would *wear something like that to burn a place down.* Yellow hoodie, a snake on the back, blood-red roses on the sleeves. It is Jules for sure, even though the photograph was taken by a surveillance camera, with its gritty quality. Even though it's murky like the pictures tabloids used to claim were of the Loch Ness monster, or the snaps of Elvis eating pancakes in a roadside diner. Jules, under the headline 'OPP Releases Images of Suspect in Restaurant Fire'. Franco doesn't have to pick up the phone, doesn't have to answer *If anyone has information please contact,* but he will. He does. He wants to be the one.

Cedar can't sleep. The hotel room is so cold it hurts. Franco, over dinner earlier—at the casino's steakhouse, knife half-sunk in a slab of charred octopus, a thorny salad on the side—said, *Maybe you need to see a doctor.* But Cedar already had. She remembers the doctor's clean, even nails, and his medicinal cologne: bloodroot and crushed aspirin. His eyes never leaving the screen of the laptop as he quickly clicked the keys. A bottle of pills: Take twice daily for nerves. She swallowed them for a week and hated them, the way they muddled her, left her sluggish and damp. So stunned she couldn't catch her own thoughts long enough to dwell on anything, and she forgot to wash the dishes, get the groceries. When she does buy groceries, she leaves them out on the counter so long that the ice cream melts. Instead she lay in bed all day, reading about Moth-man, crop circles, and ghosts. All her thoughts lumbered slowly on, drowsy sheep, just ahead of her always, leaving her mind a flat, empty field. A void is not peace. Nothingness is not the same as happiness. She threw the pills out. *Because you always want the quick fix,* Franco said.

At the steakhouse, Cedar had ordered macaroni and cheese.

You could try the baked escargot—

It's like chewing on someone's used gum, Cedar had said. Franco shrugged, sipped his mineral water garnished with a basil leaf.

Now Franco is asleep in their hotel room, television on. The blue light flickers over his back, spine, and shoulder blades, a topography she had committed to memory years ago. Before, they would have both been awake, watching *Attack of the Giant Leeches* or *Atom Age Vampire* or Cedar's favourite, *The Reptile*—she still loves the cold-blooded curse of the girl in the film, a village maid, a doctor's daughter. At dusk, she'd shed her dress and skin for scales.

Cedar hasn't really thought about that girl in a long time. Now she wants to be her, shifting from girl to monster, sliding in and out of her corset, ever unsuspected. Sinking teeth deep into throats.

She stands by the windows overlooking Riverside Drive and Detroit's luminous Art Deco skyline—Cadillac Tower, the Fisher Building, One Woodward Avenue. She looks east to see if she can glimpse Franco's restaurant, Arrivederci, though it would be closed now, anyway; they aren't open this late. Sees nothing but the shingle collage of rooftops and dark, blotting trees, the sky in the east bright with a strange, searing light.

Before the fire ever starts, there is Jules.

Franco would never have hired Jules, but Angela, his best waitress, had said *please,* sliding his resumé over the bar. *He's my cousin.* So Franco gave him a chance.

Jules turned out all right. Punctual, energetic, a good waiter. Customers loved him. There is no accounting for taste, Franco sadly knows. People love canned noodles, too, and that is basically Jules: the human equivalent of Zoodles. This knowledge gives Franco a small but physical pain, like when people use artificial vanilla instead of pure vanilla extract and claim that it's good enough.

Jules is Jägerbombs and diamond earrings. Jules is putting flame decals on a good car. Jules is Taco Bell for breakfast. Jules has theories on Bigfoot. In school, Jules drank cough syrup and failed chemistry while Franco was star of the school's hockey team, scoring hat tricks and then scholarships to study business and the culinary arts.

Jules is lucky.

These are all the things Franco believes of Jules, and some of them are true, or all of them. Now Jules is also an arsonist. Franco knows this, too.

When he calls the police, Franco will be magnanimous. He won't press charges for the stolen ring.

When you start letting smeared mascara cake up under your eyes after you cry, that's when you know you have a problem. Cedar knows it, but she doesn't clean her face. She stays like that, looking like 1970s Ozzy Osbourne singing 'Paranoid', lashes gummed together, batwing-thick.

Cedar goes to family dinners with Franco, to his parents' house on Lake St. Clair with its water views, dock, mahogany hardwood, and sculpted glass fixtures. Everyone talks about keeping their weight down and their bank account up. Franco's mother, Carmen, owns a yoga studio and posts about #fitnessgoals. She still fits into her wedding dress from 1979—snow-white organza, an impeccable silhouette. She likes to bring it up over dinner, and also how Cedar doesn't fit into her own wedding dress anymore, a beaded A-line in ivory.

Cedar says, 'If I had got the corset back I would,' but she had gone instead for the row of little white buttons up the back, a beaded spine. Carmen says, 'That isn't the point. The point is that you should take care of yourself.' Then she says, 'Franco, this dinner,' which is cold-water lobster tail and drawn butter, wilted arugula, blistered tomatoes. Franco clarifies his own butter. 'Every time you outdo yourself.' She lays down her knife, stainless steel flatware in matte gold, on the linen napkin. Cedar thinks of *The Great Gatsby*, thinks this is what would have happened if Tom had married Myrtle. Not a romance or a tragedy, just long, slow disquiet, and Myrtle forever mixing up the salad fork with the fish fork. Or maybe she would have learned, one day, to discern the difference.

———————

'At least Cedar's the one that got pregnant,' Shay says.

'What does that mean?' Franco doesn't want to go to Cedar's family dinners, either.

Shay only smiles, picks at her salt-roasted-beet salad.

Franco knows what it means: it means Angela. Just because Shay saw them that one time together, at Devonshire Mall, she thinks she knows, but she doesn't. Like her sister, she eats salad with the wrong fork. The vinaigrette is wildflower honey, but Franco wonders why he bothers. He might as well just bring a bottle of ranch. There is no point trying to help Cedar, he thinks. She should want to better herself, but lacks the aspiration. It would be like trying to teach Cedar the proper way to *mise en place*. But she cooks the way she lives: haphazard, untidy. Disordered, even, you could say.

———————

When Franco thinks about Cedar, he thinks about the good life he's given her: the beautiful house, the sunken living room with the view of the river, the new sectional sofa (leather, in a grey shade called *fin*). It makes him happy. He understands why people start sanctuaries for sick tigers, for greyhounds retired from racing. It's a nice feeling. It's not his fault she never stopped wanting to stay up all night watching *Creature from the Black Lagoon*. It's not his fault he grew up. Just like Angela is not his fault, or not entirely. But Franco has ambition; he will keep trying to culture Cedar, gradually, with patience. Like an oyster, he will do the gritty work, make the revisions. He will turn a bothersome grain of sand into a luminous pearl.

A late-summer storm snaps the stalks of Cedar's sunflowers. They bend at the waist, their faces kissing the dirt. She goes out with a pair of scissors and some duct tape, tapes their long stems one by one back up against the wall.

Franco's car pulls into the driveway. He gets out, stares at Cedar for a moment, standing there in her pyjama pants, roll of tape around her wrist.

'What are you doing?'

'Fixing the sunflowers.'

'With duct tape?'

'It's working.'

'That's not the point.' He never liked sunflowers—lowbrow, flashy flowers. He would like to see something small, neat, disease-resistant—a sleek green boxwood, sharply trimmed. 'I give you this beautiful home,' he says. 'And all you do is wreck it.'

When Cedar answers the door she doesn't recognize Jules at first. He is standing there in a yellow hoodie with a snake on the back, hands in his pockets, waiting. At the restaurant, he's always in his button-up shirt, white, starched, the collar crisply ironed.

'Is Franco home?'

'No.'

'I'm supposed to pick up his extra keys.'

'He left them on the table.'

He takes off his hoodie. His t-shirt is flashy and floral, like seventies wallpaper. Cedar can see the tattoos he covers for work—roses, black stars, the start of angel wings over his upper arms. She can just see the first few feathers. All morning she has been crying on and off. *Hormones*, Franco says. When she was still working, at the insurance office, she'd had to attend a workshop about interpersonal relationships and problem solving. The only thing she remembers is the speaker saying you could stop yourself from crying if you kept your butt clenched. Cedar experiments, and it works, sort of. But the problem is you can't go around clenched all day. Cedar knows this. She's tried.

Jules can see the dried tear tracks on her face, like the rivulets rain leaves on dusty glass. 'I like your sunflowers,' he says.

'Thank you.' She pulls her sweater over the slope of her stomach, rubs the back of her hand at the mascara under her eyes. The television is on, *The Reptile*. 'Did you want to come in?'

'All right,' he says. 'I don't work for an hour.'

Jules walks inside. Cedar shuts the door. 'Can I see your wings?' she asks.

———————

Jules is showing up late to work, calling in sick—things he has never done. Franco pulls him aside before his shift starts. 'What's going on?'

Jules thinks Franco is emotionally scarred, or maybe just emotionally stunted. He is handsome in a sociopathic way, with a cool blankness to him, like the smooth, numberless face of his gold watch.

'I know, I'm sorry, I've been losing track of time. I've been seeing this girl —'

Franco laughs. 'You're a hopeless romantic.'

'Hopeful romantic.'

'That isn't the saying.'

Jules says, 'I'm rewriting the language. But she's with someone else.' His white dress shirt is unbuttoned and Franco can see an Ed Hardy shirt underneath, a tiger amidst roses, *forever* in tattoo font on an unfurling banner. Shirts like that were a joke ten years ago, and now they're just tragic. That's Jules: a tragic sort of joke.

Franco says, 'Look, Jules, some people are like chicken pox. It's best to have them once and get over it.'

'But chicken pox stays in your body forever,' Jules says. 'It remains in your nerve cells and comes back later as shingles. It's really painful.'

'My point is,' Franco says, 'you need to inoculate yourself against some people. Expose yourself in small doses. Like a vaccination for measles. Once or twice, three times, maximum. Then you're immune. The trick is not to overdo it.' Franco knows it is solid advice that he's giving; it's how he got over Angela. His body is now as resistant to her as it is to tetanus.

'I don't think you're supposed to talk about people that way,' Jules says. 'Like a virus. Like a disease.'

Franco shrugs. 'All right, Jules,' he says. 'I just need you to show up for work on time.'

In September, Franco sits with Angela in his car.

'Thanks for hiring Jules,' she says. 'This job has helped him so much. He's happy. And he's seeing someone now, too.'

'There's someone for everyone, I guess.'

'I want to meet her, but he won't let me. He keeps saying not yet. It's complicated. She's pregnant—'

'Jules is going to be a father?'

Angela says, 'It's someone else's.' She is dressed for work still, in a knee-length black pencil skirt, her white blouse cuffed tidily at her elbows. Muted grey, newly manicured nails. Two tiny gold bars of her earrings, slim as pins. A thin line of gold over her collarbone where the necklace he gave her catches the light.

That would be just like Jules, Franco thinks, getting involved with a woman pregnant with another man's baby. Jules is so messy, like the people who populated the trashy daytime talk shows on every afternoon in the nineties. Franco can imagine the kind of girl who would end up with Jules, but doesn't want to say it. It's a nice night—why ruin it? Maybe Cedar is right, anyway. Maybe he is too negative sometimes. Angela lays her head down on his shoulder, flicks a finger at the radio. Earlier they worked on a new recipe— tagliatelle in a brown butter sauce, with parsnips and fried sage. Angela chopped the herbs; now she smells like sage and he loves it.

'He says one of these days, though, he wants me to meet her. That we can get together and watch her favourite movie. Something called *The Lizard*?'

'*The Lizard*?'

'Oh, no, I mean *The Reptile*.'

———————

A local magazine interviewed Franco, once, about his restaurant. Cedar flips through the slick pages till she finds him, photographed standing beside his beloved herb garden, in stiff, buttoned-up white, like a chef. The interviewer asked Franco to name his favourite spice. Franco had demurred; he could never choose, he said. It would be like asking a parent to name their favourite child. *Say black salt*, Cedar thinks. *Say cardamom. Say anything at all.* In the photograph he smiles and the sunlight almost mellows him. The rosemary and lemon balm fade into a gentle green background. Cedar notices his good posture, his steady shoulders, but she also sees beyond the smile, sees the tension that tightens his jaw. She understands who he is. Franco had worried about rain that day, before the photographer arrived, but in the end it had all been all right. In the picture, the sky is a quiet, cloudless blue.

———————————

Franco tells himself he should not be surprised. Cedar and Jules are scavengers, and scavengers take what they can get. They are vultures picking at bone, shiny beetles in dead leaves, foxes by the roadside licking blood from their fur.

Cedar isn't the only one who wants to cry all day, but the difference between them is that he doesn't allow himself to yield to it, to make a hobby of his regrets and miseries. There are other differences, too, but Franco considers this the most crucial one. Maybe this isn't the life he always wanted, either, but he made the most of it. Maybe he didn't want to take on the restaurant, his father's business, work seven days a week. Maybe he wanted to be a lawyer or a pastry chef or just a lazy deadbeat like Jules, blowing his paycheques on tattoos and Red Bull. Or maybe this is what he would have chosen anyway, in the end, but it's the choice itself he wanted, and it's the choice he never got.

Now he's sitting in his office just behind the bar, waiting for Jules. He already has the fuel, and he has been saving newspapers for a week. He'd ducked into the library on his lunch break to do a little discreet research. He knows better than to Google the bad things you're about to do, learned as much from his old *Law & Order* marathons with Cedar.

When Jules shows up he looks nervous, but Franco smiles, offers him a glass of mineral water, gestures to a chair. It isn't about Jules wanting to be with Cedar, Franco tells himself. It's about Jules wanting to be like him, to live like he does, to have what he has.

That's understandable, almost forgivable. Franco's doing him a kindness, giving him an opportunity.

'You wanted to talk to me?' Jules moves to take a sip, spills water down his shirt.

'I want us to make a trade,' Franco says. 'I already know what you want. Now I'll tell you what I need.' He twists the wedding ring off his finger, fourteen-karat gold, offers it. 'A certain percentage of the insurance money, too, of course, when all that is sorted out.'

Jules doesn't sit, but he listens. When he turns to leave, he shakes Franco's hand, takes the duffle bag Franco has prepared.

Franco walks Jules to the door. 'The key is multiple ignition points,' he says.

———————————

Franco has read the criminal code. He expects Jules will get four years, five, maybe, or two years less a day. He feels like a mad scientist or Dracula, the villain in one of Cedar's horror movies, regarding his creation with sorrow and with pride. He has made a monster, but he has also given Jules a kind of purpose. In a way, it's the second time Franco has given Jules a chance. People like Jules always had urges towards criminality and self-destruction. It is raw talent Franco senses, the potential for a vocation. When Jules gets out, he could make a career of this, given enough ambition.

It's what Franco would do, if he could.

LAST SUMMER

The summer we turn nineteen, we are like the Velveteen Rabbit: we wait for a boy to love us enough to make us real.

We are unkind in love, and we are loved unkindly. We go out at night in floral combat boots, tattoo chokers, slip dresses. Or in jeans, tight and low as they can go on the hips, with platform sandals. Or pink-tinted sunglasses and rainbow-striped crop tops and Skechers, like the ones Britney Spears paired with a denim maxi skirt in the magazine ads in *YM*, between articles about pop stars and purity rings. Who wears what? Sadie or Rhea or myself, it doesn't matter. We trade frosted lipstick and clothes. We sleep over all summer at each other's houses, pass out in the same bed still wearing our makeup. We share everything. Like an octopus, we are one body with three hearts. We are the spheres of Newton's Cradle—we look separate, but always move together. What happens to one of us happens to all of us.

There are 338 species of hummingbirds. Their names are striking—sunangel, glittering-throated, violetear. Brilliant, they shine with gemmed agility, their needs so wild they fall into a state called torpor, in which they're not dead but not alive, not really, a sort of hibernation where their hearts calm down, their breathing slows, and they finally get a chance to rest.

We drink in Sadie's basement, sitting on the dusty-rose sofas. Sadie and Rhea and me, our hair flat-ironed to an oily sleekness. Our silver hoop earrings and heart-shaped rhinestone necklaces from Ardene, glitter eyeshadow pressed onto eyelids under brows we tweak constantly until they are only thin dark crescents. Sadie loves *Sex and the City* so we drink candy-pink cosmos in martini glasses. We're sapphire-spangled, and we drink till we're ruby throated. We avoid the kitchen, where the wallpaper border of yellow flowers closes in on us, cages us, the same motif repeated over and over. We prefer instead the basement, dwelling among shelves of her father's racquetball trophies and music posters. On the wall by the stairs is a framed painting of Marilyn Monroe, James Dean, and Elvis, playing pool together in a bar, rockabilly trinity. Elvis staring at Marilyn, whose lips are perpetually parted in surprise, eyebrows arched. She is wearing the pink satin gown and elbow-length gloves she wore to sing 'Diamonds Are a Girl's Best Friend'. James Dean looking out over the green felt of the pool table at us, mournfully, sculpted blond pompadour and jeans cuffed perfectly. Where are they, we want to know. Sadie says they're in heaven, but sometimes I wonder.

Arthur and I walk along Erie Street in the afternoons, when we're not in classes. Past a garden fence painted with the Italian flag, past shops selling Communion dresses and silk shawls, past Italia Bakery, wedding cakes in the windows, lacy with sugar flowers. We go to our own class (American Literature for me, Later Romanticism for him), and also usually to each other's. The World Cup is happening that summer, and the cafés on Erie Street are showing the games. We drink espresso from small blue china cups with matching saucers in a gold triangle pattern, even though I don't like the taste. Arthur does, and I feel like I should, so that summer I try to make myself love it.

'I had this weird dream last night.'

Arthur rolls his eyes. 'Are you one of those people who thinks dreams mean anything?'

I am, but I shrug. He has foam from the espresso on his upper lip and I want to say something or reach across the green marble table and wipe it away with a napkin, or my hand, even. 'I don't usually remember my dreams, that's all.'

'Go ahead and tell me.'

The inner rims of the little cups shine gold. On the television, Italy scores against the US. The crowd in the café cheers, *forza Azzuri*.

'I woke up in the Bluebell Motel.'

'I don't know what that is.' Arthur isn't from Windsor, and he doesn't like Windsor, even after three years here. He has already decided he won't stay when he graduates from university.

'It's just, like, this dirty motel by my house.'

'Have you been there?'

'No, I just see it all the time. Anyway, I dreamed I woke up in one of the rooms there. But it felt so real. Like I could feel the dampness of the sheets, and when I pushed them back, all these insects came crawling out, hundreds of them. Cockroaches and centipedes and beetles.'

'Lucy, that's disgusting.' Arthur grimaces. 'Who were you with?'

'No one,' I say. 'I was alone.'

'Yeah, right. You were probably with Everett.'

Everett is in our American Literature class. He has long beachy hair and a beard and Arthur says he looks like an extra from *Jesus Christ Superstar* and he also says that I love him. Everett wears a lilac-coloured blazer over an old blue button-up and bracelets with beads made from coconut wood. He puts up his hand to talk about the book we are reading right now, which is *Jazz*. He likes to talk about the bird motif and once he read aloud the lines about not falling in love, but rising in it. Arthur is watching so I remind myself to swallow.

'I wasn't,' I say, irritated that he thinks I am keeping something back, a ridiculous secret. 'If I was, I would tell you.'

'I'm sure you would.' Arthur places his espresso cup down on its blue saucer. 'Every filthy detail.'

Before the bar, Sadie and I make Rhea a cake for her twentieth birthday that weekend. Boxed vanilla cake mix from the little Zehrs down the street, by the 7-Eleven. Halfway through, we start drinking, shots of limoncello that we both hate, the lemon scorch almost chemical, like a cleaning product. We burn the cake, just a little, but the frosting turns out all right. Sadie finds a palette knife in one of her mother's drawers and we agree the end result is respectable.

Sadie's boyfriend, Jason, is sick, so we make plans to go out together. I sit on the living room sofa while Sadie talks to Jason on the phone upstairs in her bedroom. He doesn't want her going out to the bar without him, he says. Sadie says, 'Look, Lucy is here, we're already dressed, we're going,' and a moment later she comes down the stairs in her leopard-print kitten heels and a black silky top over jeans and says, 'Let's go, let's get out of here.'

'Jason goes to bars all the time without you,' I say, my words punctuated by the choppy echo of our heels as we clack down the sidewalk and the low murmur of traffic as we get closer to Tecumseh Road.

'It's different,' Sadie says, reaching for my hand to keep steady. She smells like lemons and sugar. I breathe in her perfume, too—Lovely, by Sarah Jessica Parker. Cedar wood and lavender. When I was still eighteen and needed my fake ID, we sat on Sadie's bedroom floor and she did my makeup so I could become the other girl, Marianne. Brown eyeshadow and lipstick the shade of red brick, pencil darkening my eyebrows. I closed my eyes and hoped Sadie would keep touching my face like that forever.

'Why is it different?' I ask, and Sadie says, 'We're girls.'

I meet Arthur first semester when we have the same philosophy class together. It is about robotics and ethics. The professor asks, Do machines have souls? 'What about Rock'Em Sock'Em Robots,' I say under my breath. 'Do they have souls?' Arthur laughs. I try to lean back in my seat so that my arm touches his arm, but he doesn't seem to notice.

We walk barefoot the last block to the bar because we can't stand to walk in our heels anymore. In the loose gravel at the edge of the parking lot we slip them back on, leaning on each other to wipe the dirt from our soles, sequinned purses slung over our bare shoulders. Shots of Tequila Rose at the bar, milky sweet, and then a man buys us double shots of whisky. Over the speakers 'You Shook Me All Night Long' comes on, first the rolling opening chords and then the drums, and this is our song, Sadie's and mine, and the whisky blooms hot in my chest, and I'm glow-throated, and nothing is better than this.

One minute, I'm on the dance floor with Sadie and the next minute, Jason has recovered and is here to take her home. 'Come on,' Sadie says. 'He'll give you a ride home, too.' He gets sick in the parking lot, though, leaning out of the car to vomit on the asphalt, over and over again.

Rhea says it is very important that men don't see you as *one thing only*. We're eating her cake for breakfast and she tell us it's trashy to curse around a boy. Even if he does, you should still watch your mouth, because it isn't nice and they won't like it.

'So you've never cursed around a guy?'

'Never, and I don't kiss on the first date,' Rhea says, serene in the purity of her convictions.

I take a bite of frosting and say, 'Sometimes small talk is hard,' which is more or less a joke but also true, in a way. Rhea sighs.

'I'm trying to help you, Lucy,' she says. 'Don't you want the nice boys to take you seriously?'

I say, 'What if I want the not-nice boys?' and Rhea's nose creases at the bridge.

'Ugh, Lucy,' she says. 'You would.'

———————

When I am thirty, I will sit in the staffroom at work and wonder how life became all cold coffee and car payments, dull adulthood. Every noon in this staffroom, where the heat never works and the sink stacks up with unwashed dishes brittle with old lunches. If I had just taken Roboethics more seriously. And Jasmine, who I work with, will be talking to another woman I work with, Emily, and she'll be saying, *We all have to go out sometime. You'll like her. She's real, you know?* And I will wonder who all these unreal girls are that she knows, and what it is that makes them so.

———————

At university, summers are long. They last forever, and even though we take summer courses, and we go to work (Rhea selling jeans at Garage at Tecumseh Mall, Sadie and I cashiers at Giant Tiger), we still have so much time. We go to Zellers and buy bikinis, or Country Time for coffee and to study for exams. We go to Glamour Nails and get acrylics put on, glossy French manicures on square-tipped nails. We watch *Twin Peaks* in Sadie's basement. After death, Laura Palmer reappears to garble through her scenes in Cooper's dreams, haunting and blonde. I love Laura, doomed by her double life.

———————

Now I call Sadie on the phone while I wash lettuce for dinner. If it's just for me, sometimes I don't wash it at all. But if it's for Everett, too, then I do. When you meet him, at first you might get the idea that he has this sort of carefree energy, but he's actually pretty uptight about a lot of things, and food-borne illness is one of them. He's still kind of a hippie in some ways, like how he uses a crystal stone instead of deodorant and won't eat red meat and how he likes to pray outside, in nature. But he's very rigid in a lot of ways, too.

'Do you think if I'd taken Roboethics more seriously, my life would be different?'

'What's Roboethics?' Sadie asks. I hear her kids in the background shrieking, *It's mine! No, it's mine!* They both have colds again and are home from school. Sadie keeps saying, *Go get a tissue. No, don't wipe your nose on me*, and she must move to another room because their piercing voices get softer, fade away.

'It was a class in university.'

'You're lucky you even remember university. I can't remember those days. I can't remember what it was to feel like something more than a human Kleenex. A walking Pollock of bodily fluids. What was the class about?'

'The ethics of robotics.'

And Sadie says, 'Fuck robots.'

'Actually, that was one of the things the professor talked about. Like, if you could. If a robot could give consent.'

'I'm glad someone was talking to robots about consent,' Sadie says. 'Since no one was talking to us about it.' I hear her girls screaming, one has found an old Band-Aid and stuck it on the other. 'I have to go. But I wouldn't worry about it all, Lucy. We are where we are now, and we're fine.'

I want my life to have a motif. I want my life to have a pattern. Instead, I feel I exist in chaos. Sadie once took a physics class and she says there is no chaos. That even in what appears to be, there are hidden patterns.

Now in a kindergarten classroom, I teach patterns, too. 'Do you know what a pattern is? A pattern is something that repeats over and over again. Diamond heart diamond heart diamond heart or A B A B A B or circle square circle square circle square.' I want to say, 'These are not the real patterns of your life. The real patterns of your life will be more insidious, and sad. The real patterns of your life will ruin you.'

———————

We are at Arthur's apartment and we are all supposed to go out, but Rhea and Jason and Sadie are finishing their drinks in the living room and watching the end of *Vertigo* for Rhea's Cinema History class. Arthur's CD player is skipping, Beatles stuck on how you got to be free, and when Arthur goes to his room to fix it, I go with him. We shared a bottle of peach schnapps, passing it back and forth while on the screen poor Judy, against the curtains glowing green from the hotel's neon sign, asks Scottie if he can change her, will he love her, and he says, 'Yes. Yes.' Now the room spins. 'I need to lie down,' I say. 'Do you?' And he does.

Arthur has a twin bed, neat plaid sheets and a comforter with matching pillowcases, and I know his mother must have bought the bedding, sweet and worried in Goderich, 262 kilometres away. Arthur won't go back there, either, after school; he hates that place, too. 'Why not go back?' I ask. 'I went there with my parents and it seemed nice. Isn't your motto "The prettiest town in Canada"?' and Arthur says, 'All small towns seem nice, but they're lying. You told me Windsor is the City of Roses, and I haven't seen a single one.'

Arthur is wrong, but that's okay. I remember the rose gardens at Reaume Park down by the river, where my mother took me to feed the seagulls, and the rows of blooms at Jackson Park, where we went to walk through the sunken gardens and run under the looming shadow of the Lancaster Bomber. And I remember the little red ones embroidered on my father's uniforms; he works for the city. And I live on Rose Street, and it's my mother's name, too. Rose. But now 'Lucy in the Sky with Diamonds' is playing, and it's a good song. I never liked the Beatles, except this song. Not because of my name, but because of how they sing about the girl with the sun in her eyes, how they looked for her and she was gone. I loved the thought of that, just being gone. And someone looking for me, still.

It is dark in his room. 'Do you want me to turn on the light?' Arthur asks and I say no. I try to breathe slack. A lax girl, like Rhea says, careless, but no, I care about everything. His Oxford shirts in pale shades, watery blues and iceberg greens, buttoned all the way to his throat. Shirts his mother buys for him because, she told me last time she was here, they are casual but classic. Smelling like Irish Spring. (Original only—he won't try Icy Blast or the deep scrubbing one.) I lean over, my cheek on the top of his chest, close enough to feel his pulse against my jaw, feel him swallow.

Then, light. Rhea in the doorway, her hand on mine. 'Come with me, Lucy. We're going outside; you need some fresh air.' In front of the house Arthur rents, we stand on the cracked sidewalk, Rhea steady where I stumble, in her white dress the shade of moonflowers, her rose gold earrings in the shape of little hearts. 'I had to save you.' Her hand on my upper arm, now. Nails painted the pale pink of ballet slippers, the same colour she painted Sadie's and mine, her hands so steady with the little brushes she never drips or smudges. 'You don't want this,' she says.

But I do.

Sometimes we see Everett, in the student centre on campus or the bars downtown, especially the Loop, and if I'm with Arthur he always smirks and makes a peace sign with his fingers and says *peace* in this mean voice, even though Everett only flashed us the peace sign once, and I think he was drunk. 'I just want to tell him the sixties are dead, man. Give it a rest,' Arthur says, and I say, 'You're the one who has the Beatles on repeat,' and Arthur says, 'Why don't you go blow him.' And then he says, 'I'm just joking, Lucy. I'm just joking around.'

We go downtown in beaded wire bracelets thin on our wrists and halter-neck dresses, or denim miniskirts and frosted lip gloss. Push-up bras and knee-high boots, the heels whittled down to needle-thin points. How did we walk that way? A bottle of raspberry wine, too sweet. Mickey of vodka split in the washroom stall. *(Don't get sick.)* Now we drink beer, bottle necks wedged with pulpy green lime. I watch Rhea and Sadie's drinks while they are in the bathroom, sitting on a shredded sofa at the side of the bar by the Pac-Man machine, watching him chomp the blinking ghosts one by one. Not noticing, at first, the stranger sitting down beside me, arm across the back of the stained loveseat shoved up against the wall. Pattern of pumpkin-orange flowers, brown leaves on damp upholstery. When I do turn to look at him he leans over, licks my cheek. His tongue on my face is electric.

Rocking on my heels, I get to my feet. Too late, Rhea is there, her hand on my wrist, her voice in my ear: 'What's wrong with you?' The truth is, I am the kind of girl who gets licked by strangers in bars. The truth is I am the kind of girl who likes it.

What Rhea doesn't know: the heart of a hummingbird can throb five hundred times a minute. The heart of a blue throat beats a thousand times in sixty seconds. As a consequence, they exist always at the threshold of starvation.

Rhea tells Arthur about the stranger at the bar, and maybe about some other things, too, and he stops coming to my classes with me. He has to study, he says, and I nod; exams are a few weeks away. Sometimes I let Arthur down in tricky, unforeseen ways, although he never says it. Like when I got my ears double pierced and he said, 'I thought double piercings were for whores,' and then said it was a joke, but still. Sometimes he says, 'You're not that kind of girl,' but now I know what that means is actually, 'This is not the kind of girl I want you to be.'

I don't go to my class, either. Nights I get dressed up and go out with Sadie, and during the day I ride the bus around town and wander through thrift shops buying Care Bears bedsheets and jars of buttons and charm bracelets with silver lobsters—beautiful things I don't need. For two weeks all I do is wander and then, there he is, Everett, walking by one day as I'm reading under the trees in front of Dillon Hall.

'I don't see you around anymore,' he says. 'You weren't in class.'

'I'm around,' I say. 'Just not here.'

Everett nods. 'I understand,' and I see in his eyes that he does. Lichen on slate, grey-green, the most perfect eyes I've ever seen or ever will. 'Did you want to borrow my notes?'

I don't tell him that I don't take my own notes, anyway. Instead I follow Everett back to his basement apartment on Sunset Avenue, down by the Detroit River. Down the stairs it smells like rose petal incense. There is a poster on his wall: Bob Dylan holding his guitar and it says, *The Times They Are A-Changin'*. We sit side by side on his futon, which is up like a sofa not down like a bed, so it's all right. Everett passes me a spiral notebook with a watercolour cover, pale waves in blue shades.

'Let me know if you have any trouble reading my handwriting,' he says. 'I can translate it for you.'

I run my finger down a page like I'm making sure I can read it. The rhinestone rings I forgot to take off look strange in the day.

You can get ten pieces of jewellery for ten dollars at Claire's; it is such a deal. The shimmer on the backs of my hands is from makeup caked on and not washed, just smeared off in sleep. Everett is wearing a long strand of small glass love beads, yellow, blood-red, teal, black, white. I look for a pattern, but every time I think I see one, it breaks before it truly repeats. I close my eyes when he puts the beads around me because the things that happen inside our heads are more real than what happens on the outside, most of the time. And I want this to be real.

What Rhea also doesn't know, what Arthur can't understand: it is sheer necessity that drives the promiscuity of hummingbirds. At the bar we put on lip gloss at the washroom sink, our reflections glowing with summer love. Opaline eyelids. Rhinestone earrings. Nail polish with sparkly chips. Someone has written in Sharpie on the mirror: *Sometimes it takes a few drinks to fall in love.* We shine like mermaids, scaled with glitter, our anemone hair. We hold hands in the crowded bar, tightly, my hand on Sadie's, a limpet clinging to rock. 'Don't let go,' she says, and I say, 'I won't.' Sadie and I slow dance to 'Here Without You' at closing time, and it is the best part of my night. We don't know it yet but we will never be bigger, or more real, than we are right here this summer. We will keep fading and shrinking, in small ways, forever always, after this.

MONSTERS OF LAKE ERIE

I saw a documentary on the Loch Ness Monster when I was twelve years old. A researcher explained for the cameras how they were searching the murky lake with sonar equipment. They could see down into the depths that way, using sound waves. Echo-sounding, they called it. Twenty-four boats were sent across the loch. They made contact with something of mysterious size and shape, but nothing conclusive came of it, in the end. Debris, people said, or seals. Nothing out of the ordinary.

I thought when you had been lonely for a long time you gained a similar sort of ability with people. To look at them, beaming out a silent pulse, and be able to glimpse the dark, monstrous shapes of their own loneliness lurking underneath the surface.

It was spring and the grass was green again, but the trees were still dark, a thousand black stitches against the sky. The cutwork of angels. I watched Mickey pop the hood of his brother's car and light a cigarette with the battery. He ran a hand through his overgrown hair, pushing it back. He reminded me of James Dean, with that sleepy squint, that aura of sadness—if James Dean had walked around in the same pyjama pants four days in a row and got kicked out of Burger King for drinking cough syrup.

I sat on the steps and breathed in the dampness: fungi and moss and rain. Beyond the crumbling breakwall, you could see Lake Erie, water fusing with light as the sun set over it. A path of stepping stones led to the stairs down to the beach. Scrape of the screen door as it opened slowly, and Sal came out, sat down next to me, sunglasses on.

'Still here,' he said. 'I thought Mickey was bringing you home.'

'He said he had to have a smoke first.'

Sal nodded. He let his brother use his car, but Mickey was forbidden to smoke in it. He still did, sometimes, rolling down the windows, careful not to let ash inside, but Sal always seemed to know. I watched him move his thumb slowly over the scar along the back of his right hand. When Mickey and I were ten or eleven and Sal was about sixteen, Sal had fractured his hand. If you knew what to look for, you could see the slight shift of knuckle bone, the scar line cutting a long diagonal. 'Mickey, if you're too busy, I'll take Liss home,' he said.

Mickey shook his head, tossed his cigarette in the gravel driveway. 'Come on, Liss,' he said. 'Let's go.'

The interior of Sal's car was immaculate, except for the days Mickey borrowed it. Mickey's presence crumbled everywhere, and within an hour the car would be littered—candy bar wrappers, cigarette package cellophane, a discarded sweater. Even when Mickey cleaned up after himself, he always left behind some sign that he'd been there.

Mickey turned the radio on, Kurt Cobain droning 'Something in the Way', as we turned down County Road 50.

'We should talk.'

Mickey shrugged. 'About what?'

'I don't know, something.'

'We were together all day,' he said. 'There's nothing left to say.'

We hadn't spoken much during the day, though, either. On opposite ends of the sofa, we'd passed the hours watching episodes of *Hoarders* and *My Strange Addiction*, Mickey not moving except to get up now and then, disappear behind the bathroom door. He ran the tap to muffle the snuffling sounds. When he came back I pretended not to notice his tender, swollen nose. *What'd I miss,* he'd asked.

Mickey was drawn to reality television featuring people whose lives were more overwhelming than his own. Mickey was drawn to television in general. He would watch anything. Even the late-night infomercials selling knives and compilations of sixties music, when they still sold CDs. Bobby Vinton crooning about blue velvet and his tears. Six easy payments. Mickey was transfixed. Even when he slept, he preferred the television on. Lullabies of white noise, the screen's soft glow a night light. When we were kids he'd even stare at the colour-bar test signal, bewitched by the bright buzz.

In my driveway, Mickey accepted my goodbye kiss on his cheek without turning his head. He kept one hand on the wheel, his eyes in the rear-view mirror. 'I'll die if you leave me.'

'You won't,' I said, unnerved by his sudden swerve, but even as I said it, I knew it was the wrong answer. I should have said *I won't.* His blue eyes cooled. Ultramarine. Bobby Darin singing on late-night TV about meeting his love beyond the shore. I used to love those sad, hopeful songs he sang. I used to want, so badly, to believe them.

———

'Maybe that's why,' I said one day as we were driving down the road along the lake, past the lavender farm buzzing with sunlight and bees.

'Why what?'

'You know,' I said. I didn't want to say it. We were almost at Mickey's place, just outside Oxley. He lived on Levergood Beach, in the same little cottage he'd grown up in, except now his brother owned it.

'Liss, everyone has bad habits.'

'I understand.'

'Understand what?'

'Your father,' I said. I thought about Scott a lot, though I hadn't seen him in years. I thought about him and wondered if he was the reason I liked it so much when men smelled like hard liquor and cologne at ten in the morning. I would think about Mickey's mother, too—Marilee, who always made us cherry Kool-Aid and Jell-O shaped like wobbly stars in her kitchen that I'd spent so much time in I had the fridge magnets memorized. *God bless this mess* and a pair of shiny green plastic frogs with sad faces and Ziggy holding an umbrella, which was my favourite. 'Your mother. How things were. Your father, you know—his negative energy.'

'All right, Dr Phil.' His voice was meaner than I'd expected. I looked out the window, at the trees dark with crows, black velvet against the white sky, and tried not to care—about how different things had become, and also how the same.

It had been over ten years since I'd last seen Marilee.

A rainy, late afternoon. For hours I'd sat with Mickey underneath the basement stairs, eating cereal from the box, crouching over a notebook. We'd been trying to invent a secret language, but we never got very far. In the end I think we mostly just wrote the words out backwards, had a system for replacing vowels.

'This is a really good hiding spot,' Mickey had said, when we finally crawled out. But I don't think anyone was trying to find us. All day you could hear Scott upstairs, but down there his rage had been muffled, like the mumble of distant thunder, something you could almost ignore. It was quiet when I went upstairs, holding our notebook. When we said goodbye, Mickey told me I should take our writing with me, worried Sal would read it. I'd agreed, even though Sal wasn't interested in us or anything we did.

Marilee had been lying down in the living room, the lights off and the television on. Before, she never watched TV, making Mickey and Sal turn it off, telling them to get a book, go outside, but these days she didn't move much from the sofa. Sometimes we sat and watched *Oprah* with her, or *Judge Judy*. That day it was an old movie, a grey scene at sea.

'A captain goes down with his ship,' a sailor said, standing against a stormy sky. 'It's the rats that leave.'

'Don't fall for that, Liss,' Marilee had said. At the screen door, I turned. Her eyes never left the television. She wore the same clothes as the day before, the same clothes, I realized, she'd been wearing all week. 'What would you rather be? A dead captain, or a living rat?'

'A living rat, I guess?'

'I always knew you were smart,' she said.

'Why can't you'—fist cracking plaster—'shut these fucking brats up? If they weren't such bad kids I wouldn't have to'—doors slammed into splintered frames—'lose my temper like this.' Marilee had tried. All she'd wanted was quiet. She'd dreamed of it. She'd prayed for it. She'd practised deep breathing and focusing on vistas of blue water, blue sky, whatever could be calming, ocean sounds, sunlight. But it was so hard to transcend. When she started thinking about pills, for her or the boys or both, she decided to leave.

Mickey had stood by the window and watched her go. The house had been a sinking boat, but his mother had been the bucket bailing them out. Mickey knew, then, they would all drown, and they would all do it their way, one by one by one.

For a year, Sal had a girlfriend named Leah who wore smoky purple eyeshadow and studied biology at the university. Her plan was to be an oceanographer. On the weekends she volunteered at a wildlife rescue, caring for injured animals and those who'd lost their mothers. She brought me there once and showed me a litter of baby cottontail rabbits nestled in a fleece blanket, and a turtle with a cracked shell. Sal refused to go. He said he hated the smell of the animal bodies, their sickness, their feathers, their fur. He would say, *Why are you saving rats*, and Leah would placidly explain about the fine balance of an ecosystem, the dignity of all life, and Sal would grab her in his arms and say, *That's why I love you. You cherish vermin and parasites … and that's why you love me*, and she'd laugh. I watched them covetously, the way Sal looked at her and held her, stroking her hair and calling her luxuriant things, *my love, my sweet girl, my baby*, almost motherly in his implausible, unrestrained tenderness. Once I walked into the living room and they were there, Leah pushed up against the wall as Sal kissed her, her arms spread out across the faded pink roses of the wallpaper like the wingspan of a bird. I started coughing before I walked through doorways, dropping my purse loudly, anything to give a warning so that I wouldn't have to see that again.

Tash said, 'They're just so different, Mickey and Sal. They're, like, Goofus and Gallant.'

'They are not,' I said. Sunday after dinner I lay with my sisters on the living room carpet, watching as dusk cast the front yard in chiaroscuro, an artist revising the daylight's gaudy work. The grass, the maple tree, my father's evergreens, my mother's petunias in their clay pots.

May looked up from her Victorian literature textbook; she had a test tomorrow on Gothic horror. 'Who's Goofus and Gallant?'

'Remember *Highlights*?' Tash asked, poking May in the ribs. 'It was a comic strip in the back. These two boys. I think they were brothers.'

'I just remember those hidden picture searches,' May said. 'They were always my favourite. Or how they would show you a picture of something in extreme close-up and you had to guess what it was.'

'In the comics, one was always good and the other was always bad,' I said. 'They were meant to teach you a lesson.'

Tash stretched her arms over her head. 'You know, it was like, Gallant takes out the garbage, Goofus throws litter out the window. Goofus has dirty hands, Gallant always washes his. Gallant saves his money, Goofus robs a bank.'

'So Goofus and Gallant are like the male equivalent of the madonna-whore dichotomy for women?' May asked. 'You can only be one or the other?'

'Yeah, exactly,' I said. 'The Goofus-Gallant dichotomy.'

'So which one is Mickey?'

Tash looked at me sideways and tried not to smile. 'Come on, May. Think about it.'

I knew who she thought he was, of course, but she was wrong. On the inside, Mickey was Gallant. He did care about people—he cared much too much. He cared about everything. And Sal you might mistake for Gallant. But you would be wrong about him, too. He cared about nothing at all.

———————

There was one night, last November, when I'd gone walking along the beach with Leah, and afterwards I'd fallen asleep on the sofa. There was supposed to be a meteor shower, the Leonids, which in 1883 had painted the sky with light. Leah told me about this, and about the writing of Mary Agnes Clerke, a hero of hers, reading to me from her book: *On the night of November 12–13, 1833, a tempest of stars broke over the earth.* But that night, when we went out, the sky had been too cloudy to see anything at all, and Leah had gone home early, disappointed, leaving *A Popular History of Astronomy During the Nineteenth Century* open on the coffee table.

I woke up when I heard the screen door slam shut. For months, Mickey kept saying he'd fix the door frame, like he'd seen Bob Vila do on *This Old House*, but he never did get around to it. *I'll take care of it if you won't*, Sal would say, and Mickey would say, *No, no, I'll do it. I'll get it done.*

So do it, Sal would say. *Just do something.*

I could tell right away it was Sal coming home, his steadiness so different from the way Mickey moved. I listened to him remove his shoes, hang his keys on the rack on the wall, shaped like a flying duck, its wings made of brass. He crossed the dark living room, sat down on the sofa, leaned over me, and then stopped.

'Liss?' The shift of his weight as he sat up straighter. 'I thought you were Leah. It's so dark in here.'

It was quiet enough to hear the lake outside, waves breaching the beach. The sound of the breath Sal drew in. Leah's astronomy book still open on the coffee table, the blue tendrils of her marginalia like creeping vines across the pages. *A tempest of stars*, in her perfect cursive.

This was how they had met: Marilee with pink lipstick and foundation on her face fine as powdered sugar under the cold bright lights of the grocery store. Thin headband like a halo over her dark hair. Two gold earrings, skinny crescents. Her new blue bib apron. Her new black slip-resistant work shoes. Her mother had bought her the good kind, cushioned for her high arches, so her feet wouldn't hurt.

Scott had put his groceries down on the counter. White bread and butter and sliced cheese in cellophane. 'Two lines on the 6/49,' he'd said. 'No encore.'

'The 6/49?'

'Yeah. The Wednesday draw. Jackpot's at like fifteen million or something. Not like nobody from this town ever wins, though.'

'Right,' she'd said. 'All right. Just, um—give me a second, please. I'm new.'

'Thought so,' he said.

Marilee had felt her skin start to burn under her stiff collar. She picked up the ticket when it printed out. 'You're over eighteen, right?'

'Are you blind?'

'Please be nice.'

'I am being nice,' he said. 'You'll know when I'm being mean.' When he smiled he showed all his teeth. Marilee had felt that if he kept staring at her, she'd be turned to ash by pure heat. When Scott came in again the next week, he had bought more lottery tickets.

'Play the same numbers,' he said. 'They brought me luck last time.'

'You won?'

'I lost on the ticket,' he said. 'Not one number right. But I met you. Lucky in cards, unlucky in love, that's what they say. You ever win anything?'

'No,' she said. 'I never did.'

'So I figure maybe our luck's all in love.'

The truly lonesome have a sort of code, written in their faces. I do believe that. Silent as sonar, as the lights of Morse messages.

While standing in line at the grocery store, a woman in a green wool coat, damp with snow, put her hand on my arm. 'Can you believe it?'

'Believe what?' I asked, turning to her.

She opened her hand towards the tabloids lining the rack. 'Princess Diana's been gone twenty years.'

'Really,' I said. And it really did seem impossible.

'And Priscilla Presley, how can she be so old? She's younger than me. Why, it just seemed like the other day she was married.'

I pictured her Las Vegas wedding, Elvis's teenage bride in her rhinestone tiara, her inky eyeliner, her bump of black hair shining beneath her tulle veil. Elvis and his pompadour reinforced with wire, his sapphire cufflinks, his cowboy boots, singing about the way he was so lonely, how it was so bad he could die.

———————

I thought maybe if Mickey ate properly, he would feel better about things. I was always trying to get him to eat avocados or eggs, foods with healthy fats that actually came from nature. The truth was we both preferred to eat trash, but I thought we should try. Sal was really into nutrition. He carried almonds everywhere and drank shots of apple cider vinegar and grew his own garlic. 'Maybe we should buy some vegetables,' I said one day at the grocery store, and Mickey said, 'Liss, vegetables are for people who want to live forever.' It made me really sad all of a sudden. I did want him to live forever. Who else would fall asleep with me listening to the Shirelles singing 'Will You Still Love Me Tomorrow' on some late-night infomercial? Who else would laugh and help me make fun of the cheesier ads—the psychics and after-midnight lawyers and burnt-out celebrities pushing pasta makers and knife sets. In those moments I still believed we could feel like everything was good again, like everything would be all right.

I was reading the label of Sal's apple cider vinegar that July afternoon when he came home. There was something called 'the mother' in it, the bottle said, which as far as I could understand referred to the murky filaments floating around in there, supposedly the most curative aspect. I was waiting for Mickey to get back from the beach where he'd gone to get high. I didn't want to go with him and I knew he didn't want me there, either. I debated taking a shot of the vinegar. Then I heard the screen door scrape the front porch, and Sal walked in.

Sal always looked good and was very well-dressed—today he was wearing what he called summer casual, which meant pale blue suede sneakers and a short-sleeved indigo button-down shirt, with aviator sunglasses tucked into the pocket. 'What's wrong?' I said, when I saw his face. He didn't answer for a moment. He breathed like something was caught in his throat. 'Where's Leah?' Because it was Friday and she always came over on the weekends.

'It's over,' he said. 'Leah got accepted to the University of British Columbia. She's going to study arctic hydrography.'

'What even is that?' Leah had always impressed me, all the things she knew. Once I had asked her about the Loch Ness documentary I'd watched, whether a creature like that could be real, and she thought about it for a bit before answering, like she was giving it some actual consideration. *We've seen more of space than we have our oceans*, she'd said finally. *There are likely millions of marine species we haven't discovered yet.* I thought of that, of a future full of yet unknowable possibilities and revelations, and felt a wave of hope crash over me.

'I don't know.' Sal paused and looked at me. 'Are you drinking my apple cider vinegar?'

'No,' I said, pushing the bottle away.

'You really should. It reduces your cholesterol.'

'I have good cholesterol.'

'No kidding. The way you and Mickey eat?'

'I guess I'm lucky.'

'Yeah,' Sal said. He was still looking at me. 'I guess you are.'

Hey, Liss, he'd called one time as I walked in the door. *Mickey?* I answered, but when I got to the kitchen I saw I'd been wrong. It was Sal standing there slicing bell peppers, the seeds stuck to his fingers. *Oh, you sound the same*, I had said, and Sal had smiled. *Which one of us did you want it to be?*

Sal went to the cupboard, came back with two shot glasses, poured the vinegar in. When I drank it, it felt like a prescribed burn, controlled and restorative. Fire ecology. A fine balance.

'It hurts,' Sal said, his lower lip glistening with apple cider vinegar. 'Leah being gone. Before this, I thought breaking my hand was the worst pain I'd ever feel.'

'I remember that,' I said. The doctor said she'd never seen a comminuted fracture so bad. They had put him to sleep at the hospital, and then the doctor opened his hand. Like the pieces of a puzzle, his broken bones had been fit back together, held in place with a row of titanium screws. 'Can you still feel it?'

'Sometimes my hand goes numb,' he said. 'That's about it.'

I knew that. Leah said he wouldn't touch her then, when it felt that way. It was like the needle-prick of a limb falling asleep, he said. A painful buzz.

'You can feel the screws, if you want,' he said, 'if you press here, against my hand.'

'Yeah,' I said, standing up. 'I want to.' I walked around the table till I was right in front of him.

'Yeah?' He took my hand, guiding me closer, between his knees. 'Right here.'

I paused, my fingertips against his knuckles. 'It doesn't hurt, does it?'

'No,' he said. 'I don't feel it at all anymore.'

At first when I touched Sal, the row of screws like beads beneath his skin, he kept his gaze on my face, and when my hand stayed, he sighed and closed his eyes. I closed my eyes too and felt the weight of his other hand rest on my hip. 'Is your hand numb now?'

'No,' he said, 'everything's all right.' For a long time after, what I remembered the most was how much my hands shook, and how steady Sal's were the whole time.

People used to believe the ocean was bottomless, Leah told me once. I tried to imagine believing in a thing like that. Gazing at the sea, deep green and amaranthine, brimming with mermaids and monsters, deeper than you could ever dream. It would be terrifying, and incredible. It would be like believing in forever.

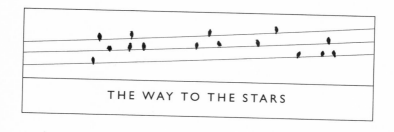

THE WAY TO THE STARS

We lived on a dead-end street. Across from us, a tattoo parlour and a shop called Sugar and Spice, which had the same lovesick mannequin in leopard-print lingerie and a purple wig slouching by the door for as long as I could remember. At the end of our street was a convenience store that sold scratch tickets, stale candy, freezer-burnt milk. It had grimy windows, a gauze of fish flies all along the sills, dusty glass papered over with movie posters from the nineties. *Titanic*, Jack and Rose in a dreamy embrace, star-crossed, unaware of their impending disaster.

Tamás was always saying how he was going to walk across the street and get a tattoo: *per aspera ad astra*— 'a rough road leads to the stars', or 'the way to the stars is difficult', depending on your translation. But he never did it.

Molly told him, 'You're afraid of the pain.' Molly, her own arms tattooed with orchids and nihilism. She wore a skinny silver nose ring. A thin tank top, black script on white cotton: *the living being is only a species of the dead.* She was blunt and beautiful the way sharks are, a sharp girl, teeth and bone. *(Don't think about her.)*

'If I was afraid of pain,' Tamás said, 'I wouldn't be with you.'

But he wasn't with her. Or he was, and then he wasn't, and then he was again. I existed for him in the voids between.

I lived with my mother in a little blue house with a rose garden long unloved by us, for years gone to seed. To the left, a ways down, were the train tracks. Coyotes slunk from the tree line at dusk to range along those tracks, looking for love and blood. To the right, if you followed our street all the way to the end, was the Detroit River.

In between were houses whose exteriors had years ago begun the long, slow slouch towards the dirt, their bones starting to show. Paint peeled like sunburnt skin. Loose shingles. Gravel along the roadside littered with skinny blue-flowered weeds and bottle caps, broken lighters and dead birds, some with wings still curved over their bodies, graceful as dancers with fans, like those burlesque performers of the fifties with black velvet gloves to their elbows, red satin peep-toe pumps.

'I was going to make dinner, right? So I went to the freezer and I could've sworn there was a box of chicken breasts in there, but when I looked I couldn't find any. Great story, I know. I tell it at parties.'

Tamás leaned back against the basement sofa, a seventies relic with a large floral print in harvest shades. It surprised me that his mother kept it, but I knew she hardly came down here. 'You don't go to parties.'

'Neither do you.'

'I know. Parties aren't for people like us.'

'People like us?'

'People who hate everything,' he said. 'We're misanthropists.'

'Right,' I said, even though I was getting a little tired of pretending to hate everything. Joylessness could wear you out. Like last week I told him how I didn't get why people got so crazy over babies, how they all looked like swaddled prunes. But I didn't want to lose the feeling that we were in something together. Him and me against the world.

If I stay up, I might call, he texted me, and I stayed up, but he never did. He wasn't cruel; he was careless, in the way we are with those who love us most.

Good times, bad times, someone had spray painted on the brick wall behind the convenience store. The broken glass shattered in the roadside gravel gleamed dully like the burnt-out stars in the space documentaries Tamás was always watching. In the summer months, people drifted to their porches, cigarettes dipping from their lips, while the dust of the street drifted up over the lawns, leaving everything ashen. We were surrounded by dead grass, remnants of rose gardens like the one in my front yard, inbred descendants of purer strains with wistful names: Absent Friends and Village Maid—Victorian and doomed. Perpetually Yours, a climbing rose, creamy white and yellow. The oil of Damask roses was used for perfume, and when I learned this, years ago, I used to crush the petals on my wrists and drown them in jars of water, a child chemist with a distillery on my windowsill.

In the midst of the neglected roses, smiling and serene, was a statue of the Virgin Mary, left behind by whoever had lived here before. Eyes closed, palms open, she seemed to emit a tender amity and goodwill. My mother recurrently threatened to evict her, but she was not around much these days. Instead she stayed with Palmer, a man she'd met in group therapy for her eating disorder. I knew by the way he sat in our kitchen, helping my mother make dinner, by the placid, conscientious way he spoke, suggesting repetition of things like *I will be a conduit for good energy*, that he believed he was a kind of cure. He tried to talk to me about some furniture he was fixing, and I could tell right away he saw my mother the same way—as if, with enough patience and gentle tinkering, he could restore her like one of his renovated antiques, repair her like a scuffed teak credenza, a vinyl swivel chair with a tear. He believed he was going to save her, but what he didn't understand was that she didn't want to be saved.

'Palmer? What kind of name is that?' I asked.

'Don't be rude,' my mother said. 'It means "pilgrim".' That image would appeal to her, a man on a journey to a better place, dauntless and committed. Once a week she met up with other women over the city market in a room that smelled of pungent European cheese and bleach, salty and sour. They were offered coffee and given badly photocopied lists of emotions, each with a corresponding cartoon face. *How Do You Feel?*, the caption read.

You could be agonized or blissful or guilty. You chose which one was you at the start of each session. Palmer had been the leader, the teacher, the therapist. Whatever the title was. All those things. I missed her around the house, but I did not miss the way she watched me in the kitchen, the nervous way she squeezed my arms, or the depressing devotion to her food journal, in which she dutifully recorded her sparse meals day after day. I knew she didn't want to but she did, she couldn't help herself, couldn't help the way she checked the sizes on my tags, the worried looks as I spooned out cereal, measured milk in a cup, 'because it's just so easy to go too far.' As if I had no idea.

Now she was mostly gone, for days at a time, at the lake with Palmer. A cottage with a finicky septic system and, the one weekend I went there with my mother, a fly infestation, beading the walls and windows, their vibrating wings a low drone.

Palmer's name came from the palm fronds pilgrims brought back from the Holy Land, as confirmation they had gone, become a missionary. He looked like a Botticelli angel reimagined by Warhol: gold curls and overblown lips, blue eyes serene behind thick black eyeglasses, retro or ironic. 'You're one to talk, Ophelia,' he said, smiling. '"Get thee to a nunnery,"' and he laughed.

I thought of my best friend Aureline, who was into astral projection. She talked about it as if it were as easy as stepping into another room. Evading your body to wander in the stars, in a field of light somewhere between heaven and earth. And then when you were done you could slip right back into your skin, like falling into your warm bed at the end of a long day. How did you do it? I tried to remember. Something about deep breathing and quartz crystals.

Palmer was still going on and on. 'Like in *Hamlet*,' he said.

'I get it,' I said. 'I'm an English major.'

'First year,' my mother added helpfully, as if we hadn't got to Shakespeare yet.

'We studied *Hamlet* in grade twelve.' Aureline had played the king. She'd worn a paper moustache and crown, and had gotten the class to laugh as she staggered around at her death scene, a wooden ruler clutched like a sword at her side. *O yet, defend me, friends; I am but hurt.*

The hopeful way my mother was standing there, one hand on the kitchen counter, in her new sundress, the bones sticking out in her shoulders like knotted rope, broke my heart a little. Her skin and hair were tawny from the sun.

'Tanning makes you look thinner,' she'd say, and I'd say, 'So does death.'

I gave up on astral projection, and walked myself out of the room.

Palmer came up to me after dinner. I was sitting on the back steps, staring at the blue ash trees at the edge of the property. I thought something was wrong but I didn't know what. I only knew I was so tired, and I couldn't understand why. Six o'clock and I felt my eyes keep sliding shut, like those old baby dolls they used to have, with the blinking eyes that closed when you tilted them. *Why wouldst thou be a breeder of sinners?*

'I'm really sorry about earlier,' Palmer said awkwardly. 'I wasn't trying to make fun of your name, or say anything, you know, about women....'

Come get me out of here. I sent Tamás a text. He replied, *Molly's over.*

'It's fine,' I said. I was thinking about Molly then. She was in some of my classes, but we didn't talk much. She was probably sitting on the sofa in the basement with Tamás now, like I had been last night, watching some wonders-of-the-solar-system documentary and eating take-out. Did they walk down to 7-Eleven for jalapeno taquitos and candy, like we did? Or were they doing something more interesting? They must have been. I couldn't really picture Molly, with her beautiful tattoos and aviator sunglasses, wasting her time in Tamás's damp basement under the brooding gazes of his mother's portraits of the saints. She played guitar and had backpacked through Europe. She had better things to do.

Palmer looked relieved. I just wanted him to leave, so I could be alone again. He and my mother had plans to go to some meditation class where you lay down on the floor and the instructor lit candles, burnt incense, and droned on about being open to the universe. I couldn't wait for them to go.

Get thee to a nunnery. I had thought about becoming a nun before, even researched it. The Carmelite Sisters of the Most Sacred Heart. I liked the idea of sisters, of the peace they promised, of being cloistered, somewhere quiet and sheltered. Of having faith in something, something true, instead of always wavering, irresolute, always waiting and wanting. 'You'll never be a nun,' my mother said. 'They won't let you wear all that makeup.'

'No,' Tamás had said when I'd told him about my convent aspirations. 'I just can't see it.'

'Why not?'

'You're not like that,' he'd said. Not cool and pure, the way I wanted to be. On the wall over the television hung a portrait of Saint Elizabeth of Hungary, known for the miracle of the roses, a blooming manifestation of the things we cannot see.

Tamás's house always smelled like cloves and cinnamon. Upstairs in the kitchen, his mother, Lili, moved around, cooking sour cherry soup. She worked nights at the casino, and whenever I saw her at home she was almost always smoking, or cooking. She called Tamás *lelkem*, my soul. Every time I saw her I remembered earlier that winter, when we'd crossed paths at church, Our Lady of Perpetual Help, in the parking lot after mass.

'Ophelia,' she'd said, 'I didn't expect to see you here.'

'I've come for years,' I said, and I had, though inconsistently. 'Remember? I had my First Communion here with Tamás.' My mother still had a photograph of us, seven years old and standing in her driveway by the roses, Tamás like a little groom in his black suit and shoes. I stood at his side in a white dress, lace gloves, a veil. I thought at the time it meant we would get married, or that in a way we already were.

Lili's mouth had twitched into a strange, faint smile at the mention of her son's name. 'Oh yes,' she said, tapping her red-enamelled nails against her teal leather handbag. She'd been wearing a scarf, too, teal silk, and a yellow gold cross around her throat. I remember wondering how someone like Lili, so tidy and neat, perfectly tucked in and combed, could have a son like Tamás, who always seemed to be unravelling at the edges, in need of a haircut, a razor, vitamins of some kind, an application of sunshine. I felt the same way myself, like everything needed to be nipped, fixed, all split ends and stray threads—if I could only be more meticulous, more like Lili in her silk scarf tied in a tight hacking knot and her lipstick that never bled. More like my own mother, who, when she cooked, weighed all her food on a slim digital kitchen scale.

'Oh, well,' Lili said. Her small gold drop earrings had glinted in the winter sunlight. 'I suppose I just assumed you were *lapsed*.'

Lost, fallen, slipped...

That one weekend I'd spent at the cottage with my mother had been in April, the cruelest month (lilacs, the dead land, memory, desire). Palmer had stood there, holding a glass of icewine. 'Your mother and I are just about to start a game of Scrabble, and we'd love if you joined—'

I'd held up my phone apologetically. 'I actually have some research to do, my Intro to Canadian Literature exam ...'

'I understand,' he'd said quickly. I could see he'd been relieved I'd devised an excuse.

I never went back to the cottage after that weekend. I couldn't stand lying in bed at night listening to my mother throwing up in the bathroom down the hall, or Palmer bringing her roses from a roadside stand in the morning. Besides, it was better at home, where I could finally be alone. I could listen to Leonard Cohen on a low, gloomy loop, mix butter and brown sugar in a bowl and eat it with a teaspoon. Outside the window, Mary beamed in the waves of sunset coming through the sparse trees. I loved all her names—Most Blessed, Star of the Sea, Lady of the Wayside. Morning Star, Mother of Mercy, Mother of Sorrows. Mystical Rose, Refuge of Sinners, Untier of Knots.

I licked the teaspoon, my heart reverberating in my chest like a hummingbird, dizzy-fast, sugar-starved, when I woke up from a nap. I never slept in the middle of the day. Outside, the scent of roses was heavy and cloying.

I couldn't wait any longer. I took out the pregnancy test, buried in my school bag.

I found Tamás sitting in the garage, watching a hockey game in a lawn chair. Lili must have made him mow the lawn because his shirt was off and he had dead grass all over the rest of his clothes. Pale chest, wishbone thin. Sweat shining on his cheeks.

'Hey, you going to sit down?'

'I think I'm pregnant.'

'Are you kidding me?' The garage smelled like cut grass and gasoline. Jars of Lili's canned red peppers gleamed on a shelf by the window, floating in salt brine, shiny as blood. 'How do you know?'

'I took a test.'

'Maybe the test was wrong. Can they be wrong?'

'I think they're pretty accurate. I don't know.'

'So maybe it was something you ate.'

'That's not how they work. They measure hormone levels …'

'I just think you should wait a few days and try again. You never know. Like, let's not worry until we know for sure.'

'It's for sure,' I said.

'So people never get, like, a false positive? You're telling me that's a completely unheard of phenomenon?'

'I'm sure it must happen sometimes …'

'So there you go. Just relax.'

I sat down on a lawn chair across from him. Lili grew and dried garlic, and the white braids hung from the rafters in the garage. What was I waiting for? For Tamás to ask *how do you feel*, for him to put a hand on my stomach, to hold me? I felt, strangely, that this was something I had somehow done alone.

'Didn't you tell me you thought you were pregnant before?'

'I told you my period was late. And it was. That's not the same thing.'

'You were so worried for nothing.' The pungent smell of the garlic mixed with fumes of gasoline was suddenly unbearable. Tamás gestured at the television. 'If the Leafs would just give Reimer a chance in net.'

I got to my feet, feeling inconvenient in a trivial way, a child whining to go pee at an inopportune time. 'Yeah, well,' I said. 'Maybe next year.'

'Give me a call and let me know what's going on,' he said. 'It's just kind of bad timing, you know, cause me and Molly just got back together.'

_____

I put on my best dress, dusty rose with skinny straps over the shoulders and an uneven hem. Perfume like crushed petals. I thought of my mother, the way I watched her at her dresser years ago, brushing on eyeshadow in pale violet, lacquering her lashes with a wand slick with mascara. *A lady never wears too much makeup*, she'd say, but how much was too much? And now I wondered not just that, but who it was who decided the arbitrary limits of these things in the first place. Steady handed, I sketched a lipstick heart on my cheek.

Outside in the garden, Mary beamed serenely. A miracle of roses. A merciful loosening of knots. It was raining; you could smell it in the weeds, the gravel. Blue flowers at the roadside drooped from the weight of water, dripping over broken glass.

Tamás answered the door when I knocked. He was wearing a

Hockey Night in Canada t-shirt, grey pajama pants. His glasses perpetually a bit crooked, his blond hair wet from a shower. He forgot to buy his own shampoo a lot and smelled like Lili's—sweet, damp, floral. *My soul.* 'You coming in, or just standing out in the rain?' he asked. 'What's on your face?'

In the hallway mirror I saw that in the rain the heart had bled into a dark smear. With the back of my hand I smudged it away, following him into the kitchen. On the table was a cutting board, yellow onions fresh-chopped and wet. The air was permeated with the smell of lemon juice, dill, paprika.

'My mother's home,' Tamás said. 'We should go downstairs.'

A few weeks ago, I'd been startled to see Lili sitting at the kitchen table as I came up the stairs, on my way home. She'd tapped the ash from her cigarette into a glass ashtray, busy solving a crossword in ink. She hadn't looked up when she spoke.

I hope you aren't playing with fire, she'd said. As if we were arsonists.

In the basement I searched for signs of Molly—her twine-and-turquoise-stone bracelets on the coffee table, her philosophy textbooks on the sofa—and saw none of her usual loose scatter of belongings. Only her beside Tamás in the prom picture over the mantel, Molly in a thin-strapped dress, purplish black with a delicately beaded floral bodice, black choker, dark burgundy lipstick, like a beautiful vampire, a red rose corsage tied around her wrist.

'Molly broke up with me,' Tamás said. 'For good this time. For some guy in her Ethical Theory class. They fell in love debating universal moral principles or some shit, I don't know.'

'That's too bad,' I said. He looked as if he might have been crying, or maybe it was only the shower he'd taken. For years it had been the same, since high school. Tamás was with Molly, Tamás wasn't with Molly. *She loves me, she loves me not.* I existed for him in the voids between, and what exists in voids is nothing.

He said, 'I'm glad you're here.' And he was kissing me, or trying to, but my mouth wouldn't open. There was a space documentary on the television, about the Kuiper Belt. A man was droning on; they were never narrated by women. We were on the sofa, his hands skimming the surface, like the way you cleaned the dead leaves off a pool. The dead leaves, my dress. Body of water.

In space, if two objects made of metal touched, they would join together forever, cold welding. They had to be the same, though. Two objects made of copper, two objects made of gold. On the ceiling over us a galaxy of plastic glow-in-the-dark stars, childhood remnants, shone a dull, luminous blue. He called me Molly sometimes. *(Don't think about it.) Molly, can you pass me the*—or *Moll, what do you want to eat tonight*, or just *Molly*, a sigh, a sign. She would always be there, a vestigial reflex.

But tonight Tamás mumbled my name, the way I thought I'd always wanted him to say it. He put his mouth on mine, tasting of whisky and blood orange juice *(don't think about it)* pushing my dress up *(don't)*. 'The universe is infinite,' Tamás said. 'All of this exists in repetition, on other planets, the same but different. Imagine another world like this one but maybe there the sky isn't blue, maybe there blue isn't a colour at all. Maybe in another universe, we're not together.'

I pulled away. 'I thought that was this universe.'

I got up. On my way upstairs I heard Tamás calling my name. In space, they say, it is always silent, but that isn't true. It's just that sometimes there are sounds we can't hear. I kept going up the stairs, dizzy with longing, with love. Love like ultraviolet light, which can hurt and which can cure. Electromagnetic radiation, like radio waves, like the radiated energy from stars, beaming on and on and on.

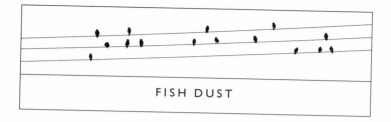

FISH DUST

PART I

My father was going fishing on the weekend with my brothers and offered to take me along. My mother said no at first. She said, 'Charlie, you haven't seen him for years.' I heard them on the front porch. They had gone outside to talk when my father showed up, but the windows were all open. It had rained earlier, and the rain smell was inside the house along with the scent of pennyroyal from the garden, and of the lake, even though we were far enough inland that you couldn't see the water.

'And when I got a look at him last week at the birthday party, I couldn't believe he was mine. It's your fault, Violet, that he is the way he is.'

The birthday party had been for Calder, my brother and not my brother. A matter of manners that we went, my mother said. Maybe she saw it as a duty. She was fond of sighing, of bowing to obligation, of sacrificial responsibility. She dealt in debts and in payments. So when my father arrived at dusk, interrupting our game of double solitaire, and said, 'Violet, this will be good for him,' she eventually relented.

'After all,' he said, 'he's mine, too. Believe it or not.'

She conceded, then outfitted me in a lifejacket and a limp brown hat for sun protection, which I had thought, with misguided pride, Charlie would approve of. But I could see that morning, when he came to pick me up, the way he was laughing, slapping my older brother True on the back, that I'd been wrong.

'You better take that off right now. That hat. No son of mine's gonna look so ridiculous.'

Even then my heart beamed at *son of mine* and disregarded the *no*, which was what I later figured out I'd always be. *No son of mine.* But then I still hoped. He had come for me, hadn't he? The way I thought I'd wanted for years.

'Look at this,' True said, tugging the straps of my life jacket, so carefully adjusted by my mother according to the instruction manual. 'Brand new.' He was sixteen years old and he terrified me. Scabby knuckles, hair shaved as close to his skull as possible.

'My mother said I had to wear it.'

'Yeah,' True said, 'but you know we're still on land, right?'

'Your *mother*.' Charlie clapped me on the shoulder, hard. Not yet ten in the morning and he already had the sweetish smell of beer on his breath. In a strange way it was comforting; he smelled the way I thought a father should. With dark heavy brows, a slight slant to the mouth, sharp teeth, and a lean jaw, he had a lupine look that would show up in my half-brothers one day, that was already beginning to shape True's teenage features. A sullen mouth, a hungry face.

'Your mother, what does she know. She don't trust me. You think I'd let you drown? My own flesh and blood?' *My own flesh and blood.* Not just music to my ears but a hymn, an aria. He whistled, snapped his fingers. Calder, shuffling around in the dust at the side of the road, came over. His dark curls were overgrown; he kept brushing them from his eyes with the back of his dirty hand.

The three of us climbed in the truck bed while our father got into the front. I hoped they couldn't smell the sunscreen on my skin. I could tell by their tanned faces and arms that ultraviolet rays didn't concern them. The day was hot already; the dusty road shimmered as if there were water always up ahead. The green trees had gone limp in the summer weather, like the sweet pallid girls drained of their blood in the late-night horror movies I watched alone when

I couldn't sleep. Which was most nights. Dracula soothing his victims, tender as he knelt for the kill. *There are far worse things awaiting man than death.*

'You ever been fishing before, Colt?'

I turned my gaze from the fields we drove by to Calder. 'No.'

'You'll like it.' He was playing with the things he'd found at the side of the road: a shiny bottle cap, a broken lighter that he kept working with his fingers hopefully, a seagull feather. I knew better than to tell him how dirty birds were, the diseases they carried. You could get cryptococcosis or histoplasmosis, parrot fever or bird fancier's lung—any number of terrible things.

Beside Calder, True stretched out in the sun. Like a lizard, he never seemed bothered by the heat. 'What the hell you looking at?'

'I'm not—not looking at anything.'

'Got to be looking at something,' he said, his voice a lazy drawl with violence on the side. Slack and soft, but sharp underneath, like shattered glass in the sand. 'Unless your eyes are closed. And I think you're looking at my hand.' His lips flinched. 'Maybe you should look at it.' Held up his hand. One finger all the way gone, another suddenly abbreviated, shot off playing with fireworks when he was the same age I was, my mother told me. Because my brothers didn't have a mother, they only had Charlie, and just look at how well that worked out, how lucky I was.

'I wasn't looking, I promise. Cross my heart.'

'Cross my heart and hope to die, stick a needle in my eye. That what I get to do if I catch you looking again?'

'I wasn't looking!'

'True,' Calder said. 'I think you're scaring him.'

I closed my eyes. *Hope to die.* Charlie hit the brakes, parked in the gravel at the roadside. We were on the southern shore. Hardly anyone lived around here; there was nothing but marshes, woods, a stony spit that ended in the limestone lighthouse. The high click of cicadas whirred in the chokecherry and the yellow birch trees as we climbed out of the truck. True jumped right over the side and Calder waited, holding out a hand to help me down. His kindness causing a trickier pain.

'You ready?' We were on the beach made up only of dead wood and shale and bone. A shoal of little fish flickered in the shallow water. True waded in up to his knees alongside our father, helping to haul the boat into the lake.

'I—'

'What are you waiting for?' And I felt my father's hand on my back. A push and I stumbled into the boat, skinning my knee. I knew better than to say anything, although my mother would have kissed it better, even now. For the first time I knew to be ashamed of that, too. My father jumped in after us and I swallowed as the boat bobbed and I watched the green shore recede.

'I don't suppose you know how to bait a hook,' Charlie said. I shook my head. 'What the hell's that mother of yours teaching you, anyway?' He opened the cooler, took out a Styrofoam cup packed with dirt. Lifted out a worm twitching between his fingers.

'It's still alive?'

My father nodded, slid a silver hook right through the thick wetness of the worm. 'Best way to catch a fish.'

Fishing on television always looked so neat and clean. I shuddered as if the hook had pierced my own skin and True laughed.

'You gonna be sick, you do it over the side of the boat,' Charlie warned. The waves rocked us. I felt the back of my neck start to burn, but I didn't dare say anything. My father cast the hook, clapped a hand on my cheek. 'It's all right. Guess I can't be too mad. First time out on the water like this, ain't it? No wonder you look a little green. It'll be all right.'

'He's not seasick,' True said. 'He's upset about the worms. I think he's going to cry.' And I saw whatever tenderness there was in my father's face dissolve, saw a sea change in his blue eyes.

The island was too far away. The place we came from looked

bereft of life. A creeping disease had infected the trees, turning them to dust.

My father lit another cigarette. 'Didn't think your mother would let you come out with us today,' he said, squinting in the sun. 'Smartest thing she ever did. You should come by sometime, stay with us. I'm gonna straighten you out. You'll thank me when it's all over.'

True smiled. Last spring he'd talked his way into a tattoo parlour, had his lower lip pierced. The silver ring gleamed in the sun. Sixteen now, but he looked older and already he had a way of speaking that made people listen. His voice was steady as a sociopath's. Years later I read about them in textbooks. Smiling, sweet-talking, until they sank their teeth in, smiling still. In Victorian days, they were said to suffer from moral insanity.

'Your mother likes to call me a deadbeat dad, you know that?'

'No,' I said. That was not a term she'd use, I knew. It sounded slangy, a little trashy. It would stain her by association. My mother preferred more delicate insults. If they'd been weapons, they'd be stilettos—slender, stabbing, personal. She would have disparaged him with a higher glossary. She would say 'absent father'. She would say he 'shirked his duties'. She would say 'parasite'. To her friends she called him 'the culprit'. Which left her the victim, me the crime.

'Yeah, a deadbeat dad. Funny, seeing how I raised these two boys all on my own. And the more your mother runs her mouth, less I wanna have to do with you. Ain't fair, maybe, but that's the way it is. Running her mouth all over this place, telling everyone who'll listen. First I thought well, fine, fuck you then, I won't have nothing to do with him. When Colt gets older, he'll come and look for me, and he'll know. But then I figured, why give her the pleasure of feeling like she was right?'

A jerk on the line and my father kept his beer between his knees, began reeling in. When the fish broke the surface of the water it startled me.

'A yellow perch,' Calder said, looking at me. As if he knew I wouldn't be able to name it.

Charlie gripped the fish and tore the thin hook from its mouth. The blood astonished me. I never thought that fish could bleed. I imagined once hooked they died neatly, gave up without a struggle. And then the other cooler was opened, the yellow perch dropped down.

My father said, 'Best fish you can get out here.'

The wet thump of the fish came from inside the cooler like a beating heart, flop of fins, tail beating against ice.

I said, 'What are you going to do with it?'

Charlie laughed. He shook his head and looked towards True, and my brother laughed too. 'Gut and fry it, that's what. What the hell would you do with perch? If you're good, I'll teach you how to clean 'em. Show you how to use a knife.'

'I mean, we just wait until it ... dies, inside there?'

Charlie looked at me like I'd spoken a foreign language. I guess mercy was one, to him. 'Yeah, that's what I was planning on. Ain't gonna take long.'

Another wet thump. True opened the lid. 'Here,' he said, 'take a good look.'

I hadn't dreamed there'd be so much blood—pale watery red and mixing with the melting ice. I felt something in my throat catch, a hot wash of nausea. And every time I thought it was over, another thud.

'Maybe there's something you can do,' I said, my voice a quiver I didn't even recognize. 'I think it's in pain.'

Charlie spat, wiped his lips. 'Fish don't feel nothing.'

'Why don't you just kill it,' Calder said.

'What's wrong with you?' Charlie flicked his cigarette into the lake.

'Well,' Calder said, 'why let it suffer? And it's making Colt upset.'

True said, 'Why don't you let Colt kill it then?'

I couldn't stop myself. 'No!'

True's smile slit across his face, ear to ear. 'I think you should make him do it.'

The same childish, gruesome vow looped through my head over and over. *Cross my heart and hope to die. Hope to die. Hope to die.* Dracula kissing the throats of his victims. *There are far worse things awaiting man than death.*

True said, 'I think it's dead,' tilted the cooler so I could see the yellow perch on the ice, flapping once, twice, limp, scales missing in places now, mashed into ice. True stuck his finger in a smear of blood, rubbed it across the palm of my hand. 'There you go.'

And I couldn't help myself. I gagged and got sick all over my lap. The oatmeal and milk my mother had made for breakfast dripped down my chin.

My father slapped me with the back of his hand, wiped it clean on his jeans. 'Don't even got the heart to hit you, really. We're going home.'

True scowled. 'What the hell?'

'We're going home,' he said. 'I can't take any more of this. We gonna sit out here in the sun all day so he can cry his eyes out every time we hook a fish? Makes me sick to my stomach.'

'Thanks a lot, Colt.'

'Maybe you shouldn't have wiped the blood on him,' Calder said. He'd taken off his shirt, dabbed at the vomit on my face.

True smacked his hand away. 'You ain't his mom, knock it off. Quit babying him.'

'Ain't even your fault, really.' Closer to shore, Charlie stopped the boat, jumped out with a splash. True followed. 'It's your mother who made you this way, keeping you from me all these years. I could have helped you. I'm gonna have a talk with her.' Calder climbed over the side of the boat, held out his hand to me.

I stood by the side of the road while my father and True hitched the boat to the truck again, vomit down the front of my t-shirt. True climbed in the front seat of the truck and our father came around to where I stayed with Calder by the ditch.

'Get in the back,' he said. 'Calder, not you. No, you're walking. Ain't getting in my truck smelling like puke, snot all over your face. No son of mine, acting like this. Your mother's fault, but I'm gonna talk to her. She don't even give you my name. She ashamed of me? Answer me, Colt. I ain't good enough for her or something?'

'No—no.'

'Calling me a deadbeat dad—'

'She *doesn't.*'

'Yeah? Then what she tell you about me, anyway? Can't even give me an answer, can you? Well, I know, even if you keep your mouth shut. I know what she says. What she's like. Thinks she's too good for me. You too good for me, too? Maybe it's been you, all these years, who don't want to see me. Shameful. A boy don't want to see his own father. Your mother acting like she don't even know me. Now you think you're too good for me. Well I got news for you, Colt. Apple don't fall too far from the tree. And as for your mother, acting like she don't even know me, can't even remember my name, how's she think you got here, anyway?' And he was laughing now, and True was laughing too. 'She wants to pretend she's all high and mighty, but here you are. Living proof of who she really is. You walk on home and think of that.'

Calder said, 'I'll walk home with Colt.'

Charlie slapped the hood of the truck. 'Suit yourself.' He climbed in, slammed the door. True had the radio on: Korn singing 'Freak on a Leash'. Music I wasn't allowed to listen to, anyway.

Calder still had his t-shirt off. Standing there, he was small as me. I wondered where his mother had gone. How she could leave him with Charlie.

'He doesn't mean anything by it,' Calder said, as we started walking down the road. 'He just doesn't want us to be weak, that's all.'

I nodded, wanted to say *thank you*, wanted him to come and live with me. Then I wouldn't always be so alone and he wouldn't have to deal with Charlie and True. But he didn't seem to understand the badness of it. I noticed sunburn on the back of my neck, the tang of vomit in my mouth, and the damp smell of the lake. Worst of all, as we walked, I still held on to the moment on the lake, Charlie putting a tender hand to my cheek. *It'll be all right.*

PART II

By the time we got to the house, it was late afternoon. I saw it as we came up the road: my father's truck parked on the front lawn, even though we had a gravel driveway.

My mother and I lived in the southeast part of the island, down a dirt lane called Stone Road, in a white house shaded by ash trees. Ditches out front, full of standing water and dead weeds. It had a damp porch, with spiders twitching in the doorway, the window frames.

I wished my mother had never run into him a month ago, at the island's only grocery store. We would never have gone to Calder's birthday, then. She had been buying milk and soap, and Charlie had needed cigarettes. *He should have bought some soap*, my mother told me later. She washed her hands ritually and so they always smelled like lemon, cold and tartly clean. My mother disapproved of him, of his careless and dirty hands, his cigarettes and his stained teeth, but I could tell these things also pleased her. They assured her she was right, gave her what she believed was a delicate sort of dominance over him.

The screen door opened and he walked out, sat down in the rocking chair on the porch, put his feet up on the railing. He was shirtless, so you could see his tanned stomach, his arms and shoulders dense with muscle. He was somewhere in his thirties then but still thin. Malnourished, my mother said, subsisting on liquor and cigarettes. Thank goodness for sliced lemons in his rum or he'd have scurvy. He smiled crookedly at me, unashamed of two missing teeth, and cracked open a beer.

'Your brother's around back,' Charlie said, to Calder, not to me. 'Why don't you go find him, help him clean the fish.'

Calder looked at me for a moment, and then Charlie snapped his fingers, said, 'Go on,' and Calder disappeared around the side of the house where the insects in the long grass filled the air with a high, scraping whine.

'Where's my mother?'

'Don't worry about her.' He took a long swallow from his beer, wiped his mouth with the back of his hand. I wanted to go inside, find my mother, but Charlie held up a hand. 'Wait out here.'

Above us, the birds were restless in the trees. The door creaked slowly and my mother came out. 'Colt,' she said. 'You've got a sunburn.' My mother and not my mother. Her voice different, funny in a way I couldn't place. Her hands went to my face, my arms, but her usual scent, bleached clean, a sharp antiseptic lemon, an undercurrent of watery roses—was gone.

'Don't worry about him. He'll be fine.'

I always think of my mother in shades of white. Blonde hair and a grey, fretful gaze, snowdrop skin. Cold to the touch. Her family came from the north of Italy, from Fidenza, a town that had changed its name sometime in the late 1920s. There were still remnants of medieval structures standing there. There still, but broken now. She was always shivering, even in the summer. On good days we took the ferry and went to flea markets in the county, spent hours sifting through dusty drawers of old silver spoons, strands of seed pearls and heavy rhinestone brooches shaped like peacocks and bunches of grapes, boxes of yellowing postcards. She wore antique lockets and cameos from another era, maybe a time she would have better belonged to. A corseted time, a staid life of tea, gloved hands, gentlemen who were held up to certain standards. I watched period dramas with her; I knew or thought I knew the men she preferred—waist-coated, devoted to decorum, suave adherents to all the social graces. A kiss on the hand, the tipping of a stiff-brimmed hat.

I thought Charlie must have forced his way in. Threatened her or in some way held her hostage. But standing there in the doorway she seemed hushed, unhurried. For once all her fussing, her fretting, had slowed down to a dreamy fidget. Not as disturbed as she normally would have been by the sunburn heating my face. She always had this wounded look about her, so I could never tell if there was something wrong or not, or maybe something always was. Now she was covering her throat with her hand. When she turned to look at me I glimpsed a bruise beneath her fingers.

'Are you okay?'

Her snowdrop skin went crimson. Wearing her opal earrings, shaped like teardrops, and a necklace with a thin gold crucifix, she reminded me of the girls in old horror films who always made bad choices. Slipped their crosses off their throats, invited monsters in.

'Go change your clothes, Colt,' she said. 'Put on something clean.'

I walked inside. Everything looked the same as it always did. All our things had belonged to her parents—the amber glass dishes, the butterscotch Bakelite flatware, the laurel-patterned china teacups. Surrounded by blue ash trees, we were always deep in the shade.

Once I had changed my clothes, I went back out on the front porch. I didn't know where else to go. My mother was sitting on my father's lap. She looked up when I came out, pushed his hands away, one from her waist and one stroking her blonde hair, which was now unpinned, loose, so that I couldn't see the bruise on her throat anymore. Her pale face and hair, her downcast gaze, reminded me of the figurine she kept on our coffee table. A Royal Doulton porcelain girl called Miss Demure—mint condition and worth, my mother said, over a hundred dollars. Cold to the touch, but I was not supposed to touch her. Dressed from another era, she had a lavender shawl, a pale green bonnet, a little pink parasol. A sweet, pallid girl. But being too sweet left you weak. It left you unprepared, without crucial suspicion. A cloudless sky does not consider rain until the weather darkens.

'There you are,' my father said. 'Good as new.'

My mother wouldn't meet my eyes. Her fingers twitched over the buttons on her long dress. Her gaze was far away, somewhere over the darkening lawn, as if she had seen something move in the trees by the road.

Charlie tilted back his beer. 'Come over here,' he said. 'I want to take a good look at you.' Reluctantly I did. The porch lights were on, veiled with webs and the little wings of dead insects—moths and other soft things lured to their deaths. Lulled by a light mistaken for love. 'He don't look much like me,' he said finally.

I didn't like being studied in the light. If this was a test, it was one I was in danger of failing. I felt I'd let him down all over again by this lack of resemblance. As if I'd chosen somewhere along the way to favour my mother's fair family.

'No,' she said. 'He looks like me. But he's got your dimples.'

'Wouldn't know. I never seen him smile.'

'Then I guess he takes after you in that way, too.'

He nodded, crushed the can in his hand, lit a cigarette. 'How'd you like having me around more?'

I looked towards my mother. I wasn't sure. I had the strange, uncomfortable feeling that the father I'd hoped for all these years had never existed at all. Whoever he was, it was not this man.

My lack of answer didn't seem to bother him. I suspected my say on the subject didn't matter one way or the other. Charlie wasn't overly interested in the opinions of others, in weighing their feelings, taking their preferences into consideration, acting in accordance. A tyrant, my mother called him, a backwoods dictator. A small-time, small-town sadist. Despot of the sticks. In the end, he did what he wanted to.

'Violet,' he said, 'I'm hungry. Why don't you start dinner?'

'All right.' She shifted to her bare feet, disappeared inside the house, leaving me alone on the porch with Charlie. A dampness hung in the air, the strange smell before it rained. He took a long drag on his cigarette, rose from the rocking chair slowly. Came closer till I was pressed against the screen door, his forearm against my chest, lightly then but with pressure enough I knew not to push. 'Came here to talk to your mother,' he said. 'Thought I'd stay and teach you a lesson—you and her both. Acts like she's too good for me, raises you to think the same. Like I'm a shame, a stain that needs washing out.'

When I was older I knew. There was nothing more predictable than a drunk. The same old scores to settle, again and again, the need to bleed it out to anyone who will listen.

'I want you to remember this,' he said. 'Remember this night next time she runs her mouth about how she's so much better than me, wants to act like she don't even know me, like she's too good for me. But when I come by, she don't close the door, does she? So I must be doing something right.'

Through the open window you could hear my mother cross the kitchen floorboards. Charlie moved away from me. We listened to the ring of forks and knives set down on the table, and then the door opened.

'Dinner's ready,' my mother said. 'Should I get the other boys?'

Charlie threw his cigarette onto the damp lawn. 'They left a long time ago. True's sixteen; he's got things to do. You coming, Colt?'

'I'm not hungry.'

There was my mother, behind the screen caked with the little wings of dead things. She had let this place go to pieces. Still dreamy in her white dress, she said, 'He should sit with us.'

'No,' he said. 'I don't ask twice.' He spoke with a drag to his words, a drawl. Sweet but cruel. Candy concealing a razor blade. 'I sure don't beg. *Please* is a weakness.'

'It's good manners.'

'Where did your good manners ever get you?' Pushing the door open. 'He said he's not hungry. He can stay out here and play, do whatever it is he does.' His voice went low and rhythmic as the sound of the tide coming in. 'Besides, not like me and you seen each other lately. We got some catching up to do, Violet.'

My mother's grey gaze flickered towards me, towards him, and then she closed her eyes. He touched her mouth, which shocked me most of all. That she would let him and his hands touch her after all she'd ever said about him, his uncleanness. 'All right,' she said with a sigh. 'Stay in the yard, Colt.'

Then they were gone. The screen door closed. *Stay in the yard.* Here, she meant, she thought I would be safe. Their chairs scraped over the floorboards as they sat down to dinner and I couldn't stand to be around. I slipped over the porch railing into the shadows, surrounded by the scent of honeysuckle and wet greenery hopping with moths. In the sky the stars were beginning to come out.

I lay down in the grass at the side of the house. Once there had been a small garden tended here, but the stones that bordered it were loose or missing and now nothing much grew. Summers before, my mother had carefully arranged native wildflowers. Leafy blue-flag, catnip, honeysuckle. Touch-me-not and pennyroyal. Milkweed, tall and pale, for the butterflies to feed on. She had long appreciated the nature of the place. At the turn of the century botanists had arrived on the island, recorded what grew in the ditches, the roadsides, the fields of abandoned farms. Snipped slender stems and peered at petals. Noted the number of leaves, sketched their shape—clasping or tendril, toothed or heart-shaped. Concurrently celebrated what they called the unspoiled air of the place, mourned its inevitable corruption.

I crawled up the stairs to the front porch. Curled in the rocking chair, I watched dusk fall over the yard, washing everything in sepia. The weeping willows to the eastern edge of our property hummed with an insect dirge.

'Start of summer always reminds me of you.'

A slow, soft sigh of disbelief. 'Really?'

'Every year around this time I find myself thinking about you. Wondering how things are. With you, with him. My youngest.'

I love you, Colt, my mother used to say. *I'll always love you. You're a part of me.* But I knew there was also a part of me that wasn't her, and I wondered if she loved that, too.

'Wait and see. You never know, Charlie. He might change when he's older, turn out looking a lot like you. Something in him reminds me of you. He has your eyes, I think. Just grey, without the blue. Maybe he's a ... softer version of you.'

A murmur, a sigh, some mumbled words I didn't hear. The scrape of chairs over the floorboards. When I looked in the window he was hugging her around the neck. Through the dusty curtains their outline wavered uncertainly, as if I was trying to glimpse something under water. I clapped my hands over my ears and shut my eyes tight till a swarm of tiny stars flooded the darkness, a thousand gold specks. A hum filled my ears. The insects in the grass or only the blood rushing through my veins. I'd seen in a children's illustrated encyclopedia, once, the shape of a body mapped with blue blood vessels and red arteries, highways trafficking in oxygen driven by a beating heart.

The leaves were blowing with their pale undersides showing. That's how you could tell it would rain—the humidity made the stems go limp and the leaves got caught up in the wind, wilting, the same shade as the girls in vampire films, in their gauzy dresses.

Their bare, bitten throats. Doomed, but they swooned. There were far worse fates. I knew that now.

The trees along the road trembled. The birds disappeared. I had to go inside. Slowly I opened the screen door, afraid of what I'd see, but my mother and father were gone. I could hear their voices in her bedroom. She was laughing, but she didn't sound the same.

Alone, I stood in the front room of our house. On the kitchen table, the milk-glass sugar bowl had been overturned. The plates, china with a pattern called bridal rose, were still out, dirty. There was a pack of cigarettes on the table, and the candy dish, amber glass shaped like a leaf, had become an ashtray.

Everything else stayed the same. The framed lithographs of autumnal scenes hanging on the walls, the brass sailboat over our unused fireplace, the sofa kept pristine under plastic—pink and green floral upholstery, mahogany wood trim, preserved exactly as it was the day my grandparents brought it to the island. Miss Demure sat on the coffee table, her gaze sweetly downcast, her pale face shaded by a bonnet, like the white blooms of snowdrops slouching languidly towards the dirt. These surroundings seemed suddenly devious, insincere. We might have the trappings of nice people, but I knew deep down that we were not. How could we be, with half-smoked cigarettes snuffed out in the candy dish and already his things everywhere—his truck on the lawn, his dirty boots at the door, and even now his voice coming through the walls.

I did it quick before I even knew what I was doing, my skull like a snow globe shaken up, and when everything settled again, I saw her on the floor, Miss Demure, perfect porcelain, *mint condition*, in pieces.

Years ago, during a summer Charlie was with us, I watched him make trips to the ditches to dump out buckets of scales and bones.

'What is it,' I asked as he came back across the yard, wiping his hands on his jeans.

'Fish guts.'

'Fish dust?'

My mother was at the kitchen sink, running cold water over slabs of white, cut fish. He had taught her how to do it, to keep it fresh, to wash the blood out. After, they were wrapped in plastic, bundled into the freezer. I sensed he wasn't really listening to anything I said. He was watching her to make sure she did it his way, right. 'Yeah. Sure. Keeps the snapping turtles fed.'

'Fish dust,' I whispered to myself. Back then I thought it was how new fish were born. I knew better, now.

I must have fallen asleep on the sofa. When I woke up the house was still dark, but outside in the trees, the birds were waking up. A thin blade of light began to cut through the dark along the eastern sky. I could feel my sunburn for sure, along my scalp and my arms, the skin tender to the touch. Miss Demure gleamed in fragments on the floor beside the coffee table.

My mother stood a few feet away, her hair like the white part of the flame, shrouded in her pale shawl. She looked insubstantial, like the wisps of milkweed that blew away in the late summer wind. She gazed at the wreckage: broken porcelain, chips of fair cheeks and blonde hair. 'Your father can be so careless.' She stared at me for a moment before turning away. 'Let me put something on that sunburn. Go and wash your face first.' I did, and when I came back she had broken open the leaves of an aloe plant she kept on the windowsill. Her hands shone with the cool pulp as she smoothed it over my burnt neck and face, until the ache dulled down into something tender, and faraway.

He was gone again. My mother drifted around the kitchen all morning, amending things. She cleaned the dishes, scrubbed ashes from the candy dish, wiped the table, the counters, even the chairs. The bruise on her neck was covered with a milky powder. *Something in him reminds me of you.* It seemed like a warning now, a threat. *There are far worse things awaiting man than death.*

While she was doing the laundry I picked the pale wedges of porcelain up, one by one. It had been a clean break, no shards or little pieces.

Outside, the tracks from Charlie's tires gouged the damp lawn. A crushed beer can glinted from under the rocking chair on the porch. At the side of the house, I buried Miss Demure, deep down under the pennyroyal. There were rituals, I knew, to be carried out to prevent a revenant. A stake, as if you could ever pin down what haunted you. Seeds or sand. All monsters had a weakness. Sunlight, silver. A handful of salt, a clove of garlic. Or sometimes only the sad and dreadful need we have, to believe we're really loved.

Inside, my mother had the radio on as she cleaned with bleach. When I went back in she smelled like lemons again, and the good kind of soap.

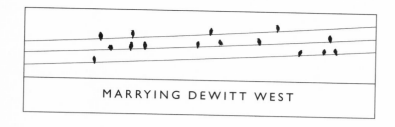

MARRYING DEWITT WEST

Before I knew him, I saw his photograph in the newspaper, grainy and grey. That's when I fell in love with DeWitt West.

He was smiling, standing on the beach, a rope wrapped around his hand. He stood with the Atlantic behind him, beside a mass of flesh on the rocks. The sharp lapels of his double-breasted suit, immaculate black, herringbone tie, moustache like a movie star's. His shoes black as his suit; they must have been patent leather Oxfords. He wore a little pair of glasses pinched on the peaked bridge of his nose. When I met him, that's what he called them, *pince-nez*.

The story said a sea creature had been dragged up by a summer storm, and DeWitt West had travelled to Newfoundland to identify the rotting carcass. *The Beast of Isle aux Morts*, the newspaper called it. They never found out what it was.

Bristles on the fins, a serpentine neck. One scientist decided it was a rare whale, possibly a basking shark. 'Preposterous,' DeWitt West was recorded as saying. I could imagine him saying it. *Preposterous.* That dark hat pulled low, grin and gaze unbroken. His eyes said he knew better. Tissue samples Mr West cut from the body proved inconclusive. A sudden storm washed the creature back into the sea. DeWitt West would not be thwarted. Using ropes, he towed the remains back to shore.

The newspaper said he was on his way to our island 'to investigate reports of a mysterious serpent-like monster in the waters of Lake Erie and attempt to prove its existence.'

All my life I had lived on this island. That's what you call fate.

'Be careful of the lampers.'

Those were the first words I spoke to DeWitt West. I wish now they had been more romantic, or more clever. Still, it was good advice, and he was, after all, an amateur naturalist. That is how he introduced himself to the island. *DeWitt West, amateur naturalist.* So I thought he would appreciate my warning all the same, although I should have not called them by that name, lampers. DeWitt West knew better. He was well educated, the newspapers said. He had studied to be a doctor (in America, he had learned to be a surgeon) but abandoned his practice. His thin fingers were still like needles, piercing and capable of healing or hurting.

'I beg your pardon?' he said. His cufflinks, his waistcoat buttons, even his teeth gleamed with money. His dark moustache was clipped sharp and dashing.

'Lamprey eels. They just attach themselves to fish or anything that swims by. Then they scrape the flesh away and suck and suck till they've had their fill of blood or the fish is dead. There's something in their spit that keeps their prey bleeding. The wounds can't close up. They never heal.'

'Anticoagulant,' DeWitt West said. 'That's what it's called. Their saliva contains an anticoagulant, which keeps the blood lymphatic. That means flowing. The name of these creatures is derived from Latin, of course. *Lampetra*: stone lickers.'

I scratched softly at my wrist, at the dry itch beneath the bandages. In the sunlight when you squinted they looked almost pretty, like a bracelet of lace. 'Have you ever seen a trout after a lamprey eel's been feeding on it? Raw, red holes where their scales had been.'

DeWitt Webb turned a little pale, then, and pushed his pince-nez up his narrow nose with one finger.

'It doesn't seem right,' I said. 'I don't see why the eels can't be happy enough with the blood. Why they need to make it so the fish can't ever heal, after, and have to die.'

The colour returned to DeWitt West's face and his teeth resurfaced, a handsome grin. 'My dear girl,' he said, 'that's nature.'

———————————

The girl separated from the crowd and followed me down to the beach. The rest of them had already grown bored by my presence and were drifting back to their homes, their families, their work. But there she stood, at the edge of the dirt road where the fraying green of the beach grass and the cord grass, thin and pale, undulated in the breeze. Her face was shaped like a broken heart. While I focused my telescope lens on the lake, she made her way across the beach and clambered up a ledge of rocks jutting out into the water. I sensed she, unlike many, had the faculties to realize, though dimly and incompletely, the vacuity of her existence. It would not be long before she, too, was snuffed out, condemned to spend the rest of her years as the wife of a subsistence farmer, aspiring to nothing greater than to clean up after the chickens and the children. Imagine living like that—your only ambition to keep a tidy kitchen. I looked upon these monotonous lives with a sentiment akin to pity, and I felt for them the profound and untold sadness that they themselves could never comprehend. Yet how I envied them their untroubled complacencies! What I would give, some days, for their facile sort of serenity, their uncomplicated desires.

Again I focused on the lake, knowing I could expect no help from these people, who would regard what I sought as nothing more than an unusually large fish. In Florida I actually had to fight to prevent the locals from destroying a beached carcass I was investigating. They wanted to use it for food and fuel. Their minds could not comprehend any greater use. They lived mired in a bog of torpidity, apathetic to anything that lay beyond their immediate gazes. Each small town, one after the other, was always the same.

And now here was the girl, watching me. Her mouth was like a red rose that had reached its peak and could bloom no fuller, verging delicately between lushness and decay. She wore a cheap cotton dress, gaudy green. She was not beautiful and never would be.

I turned my back to her, rolled up my trousers, and waded into the water.

'Be careful of the lampers,' she said.

———————————

That was the first time I spoke with him. He asked me what my name was. 'Nancy,' I said. 'And you are Mr DeWitt West.' His thin, elegant lips curved into a smile. He was standing on the beach, a camera in one hand and a black telescope in the other, his hat pulled down low against the burning afternoon sun. I stood on the rocks and watched him, my dress already soaked by the waves. Strands of dead water weeds coiled over driftwood. Above us the white sky was piercing with gulls. Every now and then, DeWitt West tore his gaze away from the lake to glance back at me. Finally he spoke, putting his camera down on the coarse sand.

'Did you know Lake Erie is the fifth largest lake in Canada?'

'Why, no. I never knew. It's beautiful, though, isn't it? Almost like the sea.'

He nodded, one hand on the brim of his hat, wandering closer. 'Sightings of a creature in this lake date as far back as 1817. That's one hundred and twenty-two years that have passed without any trace of incontrovertible evidence, without anything beyond vague anecdotal accounts of sailors and small-town gawkers. Still, there must be some truth behind such a history—something more compelling than mass hysteria or boredom. That's why I had to come here, to see for myself if I could not uncover the truth. To try and put an end to these stories, fabricated out of thin air, that explain away that which we cannot yet understand. They do nothing but staunch the mysterious and the beautiful. I came to refute the claims that this creature is no more than a sturgeon. A sturgeon—a bottom-dwelling fish that almost never surfaces!'

'Preposterous,' I said, though privately I thought the prevailing opinion made a lot of sense, as sturgeon were large enough, easily weighing several hundred pounds and reaching ten feet. Some lived for over a hundred years. But DeWitt West was a man who knew better. He was a man who knew things we had never dreamed of, here.

He smiled and turned to me. His voice dropped low, like he was telling me a secret. 'Have you ever found anything unusual washed up on the beach after a storm?'

'A rusted brooch, when I was a little girl. It must have come from a shipwreck.'

DeWitt West smiled, as if he had expected this response. He wore that same indulgent smile whenever I spoke. 'That isn't what I meant, but never mind, my dear.' With one sleek finger he traced his lower lip. He removed his hat, laying it down beside the camera along with his telescope. 'Perhaps we should leave this monster affair for another day. You could show me the beach.' His hand caught mine. He pulled me down off the rocks and hooked my fingers tight. My breath knotted in my throat. 'What did you say your name was?'

———————

When I walked down to the beach the next morning, she was already waiting there in the florid sunlight atop the rocks, like a mermaid fallen on hard times. Instead of that dreadful green dress she wore a white frock with a ruffled collar and a crookedly pleated skirt. Sewn by her own hand, obviously, and poorly. I knew what the rest of her town thought of her—their laughter, their pristine contempt, their simpering pleasure at their moral ascendancy said it all. But I considered myself a gentleman in the truest sense, and my manners and my courtesy above all democratic. I smiled when I saw her, and tipped my hat.

———————

The sky was pale, scaled grey with storm clouds over the water: a mackerel sky. 'Altocumulus clouds,' DeWitt said. 'That is their proper name, derived from Latin; the name means high heaps, or piles, indicating the form such clouds take in the sky.' I didn't see why it should matter what we called them, when we both knew they meant rain. But when I said this, he only smiled, as if amused.

DeWitt West did not toy with time. He measured every minute by his gold pocket watch. He began his work on the island immediately. He was awake before the sun had risen, on the road with a sharp smile towards the skies, as if amused by nature's drowsiness. By the time I met him that day, it was morning and he had gone down to the lake already to stand by the rocks, deeply preoccupied with his books. I looked towards the water, gleaming a hopeful blue. The waves scudded across the surface of the lake, up over the shore, then coasted back. The morning was thick with humidity, the air hard to breathe.

He looked up from his reading when I walked down to the beach. With one finger, thin as a skeleton key, he pushed back his little glasses, stroked his throat. 'Nancy,' he said, 'are you looking for something?'

'I thought you might be in need of a hand,' I said. 'I could help.'

He smiled briskly. 'How kind of you, my dear. I am sure your ardour will compensate for your deficiency of scientific study, and for any lack of knowledge on the subjects of cryptozoology or the natural universe. After all, you have eyes, and you can stare at the water all day as well as I. I'll put you to good use.'

'What are we looking for, anyway?' I asked, drawing closer. 'Do you have a photograph?'

'Of course not,' he said. 'No one does. I should be so fortunate, to have the aid of photographic evidence on my quest, but I have never been a lucky man. Fate has never favoured me.'

And he said this rather bitterly, which I could not understand, for he was rich and clever and young, all of which are fortune's rewards, or so I had always believed. But I held my tongue; he would only smile. He wore that same indulgent smile whenever I spoke.

'If so many people have seen this thing,' I said, 'for so many years, don't you think we would have a picture by now? We have pictures of all the other animals—'

DeWitt closed his eyes. 'Don't be ridiculous, my dear. I don't think you quite understand the sheer magnitude of the forces against us, against anyone, of catching even the merest glimpse of the creature we seek, never mind the overwhelming fortune of having a camera at hand, and the presence of mind to utilize the equipment. Add to that the odds of a glitch in the film, in the developing process—why, I should say it's sheer luck we have photographs of anything at all, if I believed in miracles in the first place.' Then he took me tightly by the hand and drew me closer, holding his book open. 'Do you see,' DeWitt said, his thin finger on a grainy photograph of water, a slender black shape in the middle. 'This was taken by a Dr R. Kenneth in 1934, at Loch Ness. It purportedly captures the neck of what is commonly called the Loch Ness monster. Naturally, it is no monster, but rather a type of remnant specimen from a prehistoric era which has adapted as necessary to survive in our altered climates—something we have observed before only in fossils. For example, many of the eye-witness accounts—and what little physical evidence we have collected from Loch Ness—point to the possibility of the creature's identity as a plesiosaur, an aquatic reptile thought to have died out during the Cretaceous period. Those who reject the idea of a living fossil need only look as far back in history as the discovery of the coelacanth found caught in the nets of a common fisherman off the east coast of South Africa in 1938.'

DeWitt's breathing became heavier. I could feel the beating of his heart against my shoulder, through the thin cotton of my dress.

'The potential,' DeWitt murmured. 'The scientific capacities upon which we have yet to touch. The extraordinary heights we might someday attain. There is so much in this world that we do not understand.' His voice was elegant, fine as violin strings, hushed and operatic. 'This image was taken by a surgeon.'

'Like you.'

'Yes,' DeWitt said, 'except this man was from London; he was not an American.' He liked to remind us often that he was American, and he always said it with pride, as if he had managed to make himself so through his own genius. And then his voice sharpened with disdain. 'The skeptics contend that the creature depicted in the surgeon's photograph is nothing more than a diving bird.'

And I could understand how it might resemble a bird in flight just as well as any other creature. It was a poor photograph—not much more than a shadow. But I knew to agree with anyone other than DeWitt West would be a betrayal. 'Preposterous,' I said.

DeWitt nodded and turned the page. 'And here, my dear,' he said, 'is a nineteenth-century engraving of the creature I seek in this lake.'

It was a yellowed drawing of an enormous black snake coiling through the foaming waves. Beyond its dark and sinuous curves were depicted white-sailed ships in the distance. Beneath the snake was a fragment of an article. *A TERRIBLE SEA SERPENT witnessed by a crowd of hundreds in Ohio Harbor*, the bold headlines read. And underneath, fine spidery print.

'Of course, it is a somewhat melodramatic depiction,' said DeWitt. 'You must remember it was born of the ill-informed delusions of a darker century. I am quite sure whatever specimen inhabits this lake does not have eyes that fiercely leer, nor such a look of violence. And the placement of those fang-like teeth is infernal invention, a crude and intentional attempt to make a monster of it.'

'Of course,' I said. And DeWitt smiled down at me, but it was a smile whetted by soft contempt, as if I were no better taught than the Victorians he scorned, whose dreams were filled with monsters.

'In 1834,' I said, 'two women were horrified by what they glimpsed in the waters off this very stretch of beach. A black serpent—thirty to forty feet long by their estimations, however deficient—swimming towards the land. And they ran, the poor simple creatures; science will never forgive them for it.'

I glanced towards Nancy to measure the effect of my speech upon her. I had just concluded a brief yet enlightening discourse on subjects ranging from marine biology and Roman mythology to the natural history of her very own little island, all entirely for her benefit. And though she gazed at me, nodding, her dark eyes full of light, I knew that the great truths I bestowed upon her skipped across the surface of her understanding like a stone across a pond, leaving behind nothing but a temporary ripple.

Earlier that morning I had tried to inspire in her some appreciation for literature. She was absolutely devoid of any literary sensibility. Her only experience with the written word came from the yellowed magazines brought back from the mainland—gossipy Hollywood rags detailing this starlet's tragedy, another one's broken heart, all brimming with tawdry and romantic girls in red lipstick, cream eyeshadow and moon manicures. So I sketched a concise outline of Dante's *Inferno* for her, as we kept vigil on an outcropping of grey rocks. The bleak waves, the breathless warmth of the air, heavy and static, the dark sky ominously promising a thunderstorm, all combined with the reek of rotting water foliage and dead fish on the beach to conjure up a rather morose, hellish atmosphere. 'Paulo and Francesca fell in love,' I said, 'and when Francesca's husband discovered her faithlessness, he murdered them both.'

She fixed her gazed on me attentively. Of course: As long as I related the great stories of literature to her in the seedy language of her tabloids, I kept her interest.

She sat beside me on the rocks in a flared white dress, daubed with a dull rose print. The winds sweeping up from the lake hooked her long dark hair, dragging it like a mourning veil across her face. She wanted to cut her hair short, I knew, crop it like she had seen Bette Davis wear her hair in some trashy magazine; but she had implied her father felt only loose women wore their hair in such a fashion, which vaguely amused me.

'For their sins,' I said, 'Francesca and Paulo were damned to hell, bound to each other eternally.'

She drew her dark hair away from her face. 'At least they were together forever.'

'Nancy, my dear,' I said, 'that was their punishment.'

By evening it grew cold by the water, and the sky dark and tender with clouds. The weather did nothing to improve the mood of DeWitt West, who shivered in his fine white silk shirt, his olive-green waistcoat in a herringbone weave. He tapped exquisite blue-blooded fingers against his gold-chained pocket watch.

'You must have a library,' DeWitt West said. 'Someplace quiet we can go and sit, where I can research township records.' He was paler than usual, and his cheeks had a sucked-in look. Perhaps he was disappointed the lake had been so calm today. He had interviewed a few young men in rain gear on their way to fish in the morning, and he had been irritated that once curiosity dulled, they grew disinterested in his search, even laughed at him. None of them had ever pulled up in their nets any dark creatures from the deep when they trawled the waters for yellow perch and walleye, smelt and smallmouth bass, and no one seemed much interested in the possibility.

'I am never less than astounded at the overwhelming apathy of the common man,' DeWitt West said, gathering his books in disgust, 'the absolute stupor in which these young men stagger around.'

'Do you want to go somewhere? I can take you to the town hall if you want to read through the local records. It's where we keep the library, too.'

'I have work to do, alone,' DeWitt West said. 'Letters to write to local curators, museums, or whatever passes for such in these parts. Perhaps tomorrow night.'

Thrift is the spirit of the day. Reckless spending is a thing of the past. Cut and pasted from the Sears catalogue and actually framed, hung on the wall of the town hall as if it were a precious document, a painting of some value. Words of wisdom to live by.

This, then, was the library, a dusty room off the white hallway in what could be called the courthouse, but only by the most lax definition. It was the municipal centre of the island. Nancy led me inside. It was a damp, breathless evening, and the windows were jammed at the sill. The room was steeped in the smell of mildewed carpet and dank paper. A single shelf of books, yellow at the spines, crawled with silverfish.

I removed my trilby hat. 'This is the library meant to serve the entire populace?' I asked, rifling through volume after volume, throwing them on the table, loosening a crumbly flyleaf. 'I'd be ashamed if my own town boasted such a shabby affair. How a town could be so indifferent of all culture and aspiration is a mystery to me.'

She was gazing at me from the doorway. Of course she didn't care. Her slip was showing beneath her dress, a short-sleeved blue cotton with Bakelite buttons. One white strap of the undergarment, scalloped in lace, had fallen over her shoulder. Grass stains on her skirt and knees, cheap red lipstick on her mouth. I shook my head and returned to my search, rummaging through a sheaf of papers, water-blotted beneath filmy layers of dust. Nothing here was salvageable; there were only movie magazines, disintegrating damply in my hands. 'Here you are then, Nancy,' I said, tossing her a magazine. Bela Lugosi with an ominous hint of a smile on the cover, a drained bride in white limp in his arms, eyes closed. An abundance of pure rubbish, a hoarded agglomeration of uselessness.

The building seemed to be empty, not a man anywhere to whom I might make my inquiries. And even if I did locate such a man, I could scarcely hope he would be adept, articulate, inspired or in any way divergent from everyone I had previously encountered in this desolate purgatory. I would have to rely singularly on my own abilities, a practice to which I had become well accustomed. And so I kept searching. I found a copy of *Time* from 1933. 'Britain's Chancellor Chamberlain'. Sitting in a chair, hands clasped optimistically. Finally, a suggestion of some literacy, an interest in a world beyond the horizon, and then naturally my expectations were raised only to be dashed once again as I examined the rest of what lay before me on the table: half a dozen grainy magazines devoted to movie stars. *Photoplay* and *Movie Mirror*. 'Joan Crawford's Plans for a Family', 'Hedy Lamarr Autobiography', 'Love Is a Headache'. My head was starting to throb. With tense fingers I stroked my sore temples, my forehead, removed my spectacles. I glanced over towards Nancy.

She was standing by the window, absorbed by the garish headlines in her film magazine. Her bare shoulders glinted gold in the speckled dusk, the light sifting in through a latticework of creepers which clung to the crossed iron grating in the window. In the distance, the setting sun flared across the west shore of the lake. Sunspots dazzled my vision. Gradually she felt the weight of my gaze and glanced up. Her magazine dropped from her hands with a dull flutter. I loosened my silk tie and retrieved my white cambric handkerchief. 'Come here,' I said, and she did. 'Good girl.' I took her face in my hands and began to scour away her lipstick. To her credit, she stood still and complied, lifting her own hand to smudge at her makeup. Hooking my finger beneath the loose ivory ribbon strap of her slip, I slid it lower down her shoulder, pulled her in close.

There was a cough behind us. A pale, sour woman stood in the doorway in a dark dress and shawl. 'We close at six o'clock, Mr West,' she said before departing, sharp black heels echoing down the empty hall.

My petrifaction was broken. 'Come on then,' I said, crumpling my handkerchief. It was for the best we go outside, where I could breathe clean cool air, calm myself by the water.

Dewitt West had a side interest on our island, a hobby of sorts, although he would never have called it such.

'A hobby,' he said, ridicule carving a smile out of his fine pale lips. 'That's what you call the wasted hours of some girl peeling stamps off torn envelopes. No, this is rather a bit too cerebral, I should hope, to deserve being slurred as a fad, a leisure pursuit, a common hobby.'

His diversion, when he was not searching the lake, was collecting butterflies. Moths, too, sometimes, when it was dusky. It relaxed him, he said, but he was intense about his practices. Entomology, he called it, specializing in lepidopterology. Every insect anaesthetized pristinely and classified in DeWitt West's cramped and lovely hand. When he was a student still, in America, he had raised silkworms, honeybees. He seemed especially fond of diseased specimens.

DeWitt West kept most of his collecting confined to the grounds of the inn. Earnestly he combed the sparse grass by the road, unearthed the roots of bluehearts and trumpet creepers, performed dissection on a clump of ill-fated wood poppies, scarlet petals pooled like blood in his hands. He found his paradise in a grove of rotting dwarf chestnut oaks, colonized by a surfeit of spiders. He lit candles in his window, catching moths who floated, dizzy with adoration, towards the sharp little flames. He left bits of sweet decaying fruit on his windowsill but drew more blackflies than butterflies. With a jackknife he split open unripe seed pods, sliced away at green stalks and thin raw branches. He kept glass vials of ethanol to numb insects alongside sharp tweezers and scalpels. There was a syringe, which he filled with boiling water and injected into the thoraxes of dead insects to keep them from stiffening. It was not like injecting medication into human flesh; the syringe never slid in smoothly. Instead he worked it in painstakingly while I watched in frozen horror, creeping fascination.

The divergence was not lost on DeWitt. He respected the rejection of insect bodies, their refusal to comply with his desires. 'I always thought it a terrible weakness that human flesh was so willing to yield to the slightest pressure, so ready to surrender, to submit to the needle or the knife. How quickly the body succumbs to disease, and how swiftly the cure is rejected. The body rarely resists assault, yet how ready it is to rebuff a surgeon's healing hands.'

When he did catch his prey, he kept them in glassine envelopes, in preparation for their final entombment, pressed beneath glass in cedar-wood shadowboxes. I couldn't watch their slow asphyxiation, the way they fluttered, dull and heavy, against the envelope's sides. And then his fingers, smooth and piercing, sliding in stainless steel mounting pins. 'My dear girl,' he said, 'that's nature.'

I sat with him one night beneath the porch lights of the Breakwater Inn, Lake Erie glistening behind us. My hands on my dark cotton dress pressed over my knees, on the white wooden bench while he stalked moths in love with the glow of electricity.

I had been daydreaming, lulled by the lake and DeWitt's winding discussion on vespertine flora, foliage that waited for twilight to bloom. Although it was not so much a conversation as a lesson, as it always was. His eyes said he knew more and knew better, and it was true; he did. So I listened dreamily to all those names that uncoiled sweetly in his throat: angel's trumpet, night-scented stock, moonflower, evening primrose. My shawl loose and warm around my bare shoulders, my fingers slow and sliding, idly lacing the unravelling white knit edge. And then suddenly I was shaken back into the world of sharp and painful detail by DeWitt West. He came to me, opening his hands. 'Do you see?' he said. He had caught a moth, a filmy little thing, star-crossed tonight, and I felt bad for it because even I knew it was a drab and common specimen. It was nothing to excite his passion; he had a taste for anomalies. But DeWitt West was a principled man of precision and practicality. Once he said that he was a wealthy man but still a utilitarian at heart. 'Everything has its purpose, however ignoble.' He would not let even a lustreless prize go to waste. After all, it still had scientific merit, and it would occupy him all the same.

'Do you see?' he said. 'You have to apply a little light pressure to its thorax. Otherwise it beats the scales from its own wings, breaks its own body.' His hands gleamed with film streaked from the moth's dull wings, crushed grey pearls, like dust, flecked with grains of gold. The moth's wings hummed and then lay flat, stunned in his open palm. 'A white underwing,' DeWitt West said, 'also called forsaken underwing.'

He had closed her up inside a jar. The moth was lying on its back, on a soft layer of sawdust and torn slivers of newspaper. And DeWitt West dropped a teaspoon of ethyl acetate inside. He would remove the moth soon, so that the chemicals wouldn't soak in and wreck the thin wings. Already he was writing its epitaph, its various names both in English and Latin. (He was well educated, the newspapers said.) Later the moth would be pinned alongside the others in his collection of Ontario insects, its murky wings dulled in death beside the bright glitz of butterflies. Frosted elfin, coral hairstreak, great spangled fritillary, duke's skipper—even their names were lovely as poetry. Wild indigo duskywing, spicebush swallowtail, tawny emperor, scalloped sootywing. Pieces of frozen silk, dead prisms, snuffed curiosities locked behind glass.

She would meet me each morning, and that was how it was, every day that July. I saw her from the road, glistening flesh on those rocks, like a fish just washed up, gleaming white and breathless. She always wore the same unpleasant bracelets, which she made herself out of dark shells picked off the beach.

'Why didn't you become a doctor?'

'I grew bored of healing peoples' wounds,' I said. 'It is never appreciated.'

She nodded, as if she understood. But a girl like her could never.

The blackflies droned lazily after the tide, breeding in the dankness of the beach, the stench of rotting algae and water weeds, the bones of eyeless fish gaping towards the sky. Her bracelets rattled with every step we took, the jangling wearing on my nerves. Yearning for silence I gripped her wrist, too hard, maybe; a few shells shattered. When I first saw the thin seep of red, I thought I had merely cut her lightly with a seashell. Then I saw the gauze binding her wrist. 'What happened there?'

For a moment she gazed at me. But there was no question she would not satisfy any curiosity or desire of mine. She unwrapped her bandages like she was taking off her dress. Slowly she laid bare her wrist, a snake pit of scars.

'You didn't cut right,' I said, taking her wrist in my hands. 'No wonder you didn't manage it.' I traced a blue vein down her arm. 'Do you see? You missed the major artery. It was the radial artery you intended to sever, correct?'

'I don't know.'

'And dear God, who was your doctor? It looks like you were stitched up by a sewing machine.'

She said nothing. A breeze swept up from the lake, whipping her dark hair across her face.

I licked her scars and told her I loved her.

He put his mouth on my wrist. It felt like I was opening at the seams. He latched on to my mouth and I couldn't breathe.

There was only one hotel on our island and so that was where DeWitt West stayed: the Breakwater Inn, with its wide white porch overlooking the lake. We never went in together. He would wait for me in the lobby, standing by the fireplace, in a dark bowler hat and narrow crimson tie, silk handkerchief folded over the pocket of his double-breasted jacket.

In his room were the same pictures that decorated every other: a photograph of King George V by the window, and over the bed, a portrait of Our Lady, Star of the Sea.

'The patron saint of sailors and navigators.'

'Folklore,' DeWitt West said. 'Small-town superstition.'

He had brought a radio with him, and at first he let me listen to what I wished. I loved the crime and romance stories. 'Who knows what evil lurks in the hearts of men? The Shadow knows.' In August, DeWitt West said, 'I am going to educate you,' and we didn't listen to *The Shadow* or *Our Miss Brooks* anymore. In his room at the Breakwater Inn we listened to Debussy and Mozart and Vivaldi. I liked *Swan Lake* by Tchaikovsky best.

'Do you think he meant Lake Erie,' I asked, 'when he wrote his ballet?'

He laughed. 'There are other lakes in the world, you know, Nancy.'

His eyes always said he knew better, even when he didn't say it. Through the window in his room you could see the lake. You could hear the heave of the waves on the shoreline below, loud and strong, and it sounded as if at any moment the tide might change. As if at any moment the lake might rush in to drown us both.

'It sounds like a lullaby,' I said.

'More like a dirge.' He kept the window shut and the curtains drawn.

She took me to a place along the north shoreline, a stretch of beach thinning into little more than a shifting sandbar, attenuated by currents and the waves. I knew enough history to understand we were walking on a shipping graveyard. It was where, she said, as a child she harvested the bones of shipwrecks, sifting out coins, buttons, bits of porcelain and china, tarnished keys, broken jewellery, and rusted silverware from the silt and the stones—whatever petty treasures she could salvage from the lake, dreaming of pirates and ghosts. For a year she played in the half-sunken stern of a ship before the lake dragged it away.

Out over the water a pair of cormorants plunged into the waves, jumping and diving for water snakes. Nancy clambered over a dead tree that had fallen onto the beach, tucking up her dress, scraping her legs, leaving long and pale scratches. On the other side she waited, holding out her hand. I was not accustomed to treating my clothes and body this roughly, so my climb was slower. And she smiled briefly at my assiduousness, as if it were comical. I sighed and snapped impatient hands at the blackflies pricking my neck and arms where I had rolled back my shirtsleeves. Nancy bled thin and red from a fly bite on her wrist. She seemed not to notice. She hadn't replaced her bandages and her wrist was webbed with scar tissue, frost against glass.

She stood by the rocks, sunlight dusting her dark hair with a blue prismatic hue. 'This is it then,' she said. 'The north shore.'

'And what a waste of a day it has been. Nothing on the lake, and no one worth interviewing.'

'Maybe the lake's too calm today,' she said, hand slanted to her forehead in the sharp sunlight.

'No, I am merely unfortunate. The majority of the sightings occurred during calm weather. Keep your eyes open, Nancy, and on the lake.'

I had spent the better part of the week asking after the locals in hopes of gathering some sort of corroboration, however suspect. How patiently had I explained the very nature of my search, with painfully deliberate exertion directing my interests. I showed around books depicting many species commonly mistaken for the unnatural, even those alien to the waters of the lake. I referenced encyclopaedias of extinct and long-forgotten creatures, inquiring if anyone had witnessed some similar animal or even heard mention of one. Patiently I explained how the fin of an oarfish could appear to be a mane. I probed memories for recollections of unusual carcasses washed up on the beaches, enlightened listeners on the geology of Lake Erie's western basin, warned against the illusions worked by sunlight, boats, and birds upon the water. And yet these men who lived by the water provided me nothing save wildly melodramatic folktales and the more common reaction of plain disinterest, verging on mockery.

'Sure, I've heard of people seeing monsters in the lake,' one man had said finally. 'Every now and then they run a piece in the American newspapers.'

'Species hitherto unknown to science,' I corrected. 'Not monsters. Just natural creatures that have, until this point in time, been uncategorized, concealed from our close and controlled gazes.'

He nodded. 'It's all just stories,' he said. 'Wishful thinking, maybe. Eager tourists on the causeway to Cedar Point, down in Ohio, or ferry passengers from the mainland who don't understand how big the sturgeon grow around here.'

I closed my eyes for a moment and sighed. 'Thank you anyway for your time, sir.'

Since then, the testimony had only weakened. People insisted it was a sturgeon or something sinister; others exchanged glances, or laughed behind their hands. Now ready with both camera and binoculars, I had squandered most of a day on the beach with Nancy, with nothing to show for my wasted efforts besides sunburn and my blood sucked by blackflies.

On the walk back to the west shore, DeWitt West was silent. Reddish dust floated through the tulip trees along the road leading to the hotel, our hush disturbed only by the rustle and flutter of waxwings in the yews, picking out seeds and insects. When we arrived at the Breakwater Inn, the lobby was empty. I could hear the strains of 'Cinderella, Stay in My Arms' through the half-open doors of the hotel tavern.

'Come along, Nancy,' DeWitt West said, and I did. He took me by my wrist, still raw where it was healing. Up the long, dark stairway, and I didn't catch my breath till we were inside his room and he let go of me.

He took off his fine grey fedora, undid his wine-red tie, silver pinstriped. Removed his pince-nez, gold and onyx cufflinks, patent leather Oxford shoes. Up through the floorboards drifted music from down below. DeWitt West unbuttoned the jacket of his double-breasted suit, immaculate black, threw it on the bed.

'Come here,' DeWitt West said. He began peeling away petals of prairie rose caught in my hair, brushing the sand off my dress, muttering as he did so, 'Oh Nancy, what am I going to do with you?'

DeWitt West began neatly hanging his hat, jacket, and waistcoat. Meticulous in every way. He removed his gold pocket watch, wound it precisely, set it on the dresser. 'You hear the intolerable music I am forced to endure every night,' he said, gritting his fine teeth, just as the piano notes flourished from the music downstairs.

'I don't mind it,' I said.

'Of course you don't mind those incessant, sentimental songs. Heaven knows how I ever manage to get any sleep in this derelict boarding house.'

He disappeared into the washroom and I wandered over to the dresser. I had filled an old green bottle with branches of spicebush and moonseed, wanting DeWitt's damp and faded hotel room to seem prettier, warmer, less like cheaply paid accommodation for a skein of strangers. For a day or two the wildflowers had been a daub of brightness against the dank walls. By now the leaves had darkened and dried, curled and dropped, brittle, to the scratched black oak surface, fallen among DeWitt West's worldly possessions.

There were more cufflinks, to suit all of his handsome shirts. Diamond and gold, ocean shell with silver, polished ivory. Rich shoe polish in a little tin, cream to caress into fine leather. A tie pin of a tiny American flag, all the stars and stripes. There were pages and pages of notes in his flawless handwriting, maps sketched out perfectly, diagrams of skeletons and sea creatures, blueprints of giant squids and pinnipeds, all labelled in minute printing. *The Great Sea Serpent* by A.C. Oudemans. Copies of *Reader's Digest*, article titles underlined in the index with thin strokes of black ink. 'Safety Goes to Sea', 'When I Came Closest to Death', 'Germany Would Lose', 'The Flesh Profiteth Nothing', 'A Way to Chastity', 'Pro and Con: Execution by Lethal Gas', 'One Meets Such Interesting People', 'Do Not Annoy the Octopus', 'Science or Superstition?'

I felt someone behind me suddenly, DeWitt's hands on my hips. 'Finally reading text that may actually engage more than your appetite for sensational gossip and scandal,' he said. His breath was like anaesthetic on my throat, numbed and chilled and clean. A cold cologne on his skin—mint leaves and antiseptic. Smiling in his slight and narrow way. His teeth were lovely, shiny as new money and twice as beautiful. He turned me around so that I faced him, kissed me lightly and meticulously as a surgeon performing his first incision. He clamped his hand round my wrist tighter and tighter, licking the blood from my open palm till I felt each vein throb, electrified, beating hard in time with my astonished heart.

―――――――――

She was endearing at first, the way she talked back to her radio shows as if the stars could hear, drew the lines of her lipstick beyond her mouth in hopes of looking like Clara Bow, cried at the ending of the Shirley Temple movie I took her to see on the mainland and smiled wistfully after all her dreadful Lux Radio Theatre romances. I tried to educate her.

'Do you know how *Swan Lake* ends?' I asked. 'The prince vows to love Odile, not Odette.'

'She forgives him,' Nancy said.

'It's too late. She's a captive swan forever.'

'But they still promise to love each other always.'

'And that's why it's a fairy tale.'

She was always capricious in her attentions, impulsive in her affections, and so my attempts to instill in her any greater vision of the world she inhabited were invariably in vain, fruitless as shattering your skull upon a rock in hopes of leaving an impression. I began to believe it was better that way, for to learn of the incalculable promise of the world beyond the narrow confines of her drab existence would only breed jealousy, or sadness; and she would always be excluded from greatness by her simplicity, her blind and callow nature, her unfortunate education.

My efforts were wasted. I realized my mistake, and, accordingly, I quietly began arranging my departure.

On Sunday morning, DeWitt saw the vultures wheeling over the glittering lake through the hotel window. Ecstatic, he abandoned his customary morning routine. He did not administer cologne to his wrists and throat, did not bother tying his usual silk necktie in a Windsor knot or putting on his waistcoat, his dark homburg hat. He did not scrape his face clean, as he did with a razor and cold water each morning. I picked up my paisley dress from the floor, the chiffon soaking up the room's damp chill, and put it on. By then, he was already gone.

DeWitt West ran outside and across the lawn of the Breakwater Inn, catching and tearing without hesitation his white silk shirt on the splintering wood of the picnic table. At the eroding bluff, rooted thick with stiff, dry grass straining to keep the sand from crumbling, he stopped and stood still, his silhouette narrow and dark against the mid-morning blaze.

Turkey vultures had flocked to the south shore, gliding through the salt-white sky, thin shadows scraping against heaven. Now and then they would drop, tilt, descend to the beach. A dark heap sprawled where the waves were breaking. The shifting wings and beaks of the vultures made the remains look as if they were squirming, a thousand dark feathers bright with sunlight.

DeWitt West did not even bother walking another twenty paces to where the grey stone stairway wound down to the shoreline. He leaped a good seven feet to the beach and strode to the carcass. I jumped over the rocks and broom-bristle grass after him, dropping to the sand where I crouched for a long moment, my bones stunned on impact, cartilage humming. A green piece of beach glass had wedged itself into my bare foot, a sudden sting of hot sand and blood. Even the most unwilling vulture scuttled away with heavy wings as DeWitt West approached the corpse, stalked and circled it, sharp and leanly like a predator. Rid of the dark birds hunched over its bones, the fishlike body was white and slick. Hard and yellow along the ribs, a sucker mouth, whitish fins stiff and thin as tissue, almost membranous in the sunlight. The eyes were already gone.

'Funny,' I said, 'how they always eat the eyes first.'

DeWitt West shot me a look, eyes dark and lips curled in disgust. Despite the initial odd appearance of the fish, it was no unknown creature. It was hardly a mystery, just another bottom-feeding species of the lake—without a doubt a sturgeon. He had made himself breathless over nothing.

A half-hearted crowd was gathering. A handful of men, my father's friends, seemed mildly amused by what they seemed to think was DeWitt West's misplaced ardour. Most of the island was no longer excited by DeWitt's presence, but content enough to wait around and watch, hoping for entertainment, delighted by his moments of strange passion—and folly.

DeWitt West was keenly aware of what he had become. A curiosity himself, an oddity, a strange diversion. The island thought he was peculiar, and a fool. It was in their murmurings above the beach, in the way they watched him below shady trees, waiting. He was a gentleman but they did not understand. He was brilliant but they only laughed at him. In their eyes, all his money and his elegance, his cufflinks, his waistcoat buttons, his dark moustache clipped sharp and dashing, all accumulated to make him an object of sublime contempt.

I saw the tightness in his jaw, every fine lovely tendon pulsing with his anger. He closed his eyes. DeWitt West refused to move. He knelt by the body, too proud to openly confess his frustration, to admit that green passion had driven him rushing too soon to a rather common fish, reeking in the sun. But disappointment was raw upon his face, in the shape of his mouth, the dull light in his eyes, and my heart beat with empathy for another duped by hopeless illusions. DeWitt West put on a good show, regardless. With stiff dignity, he scraped useless tissue samples from the body, took photographs he did not want. But his haughty air could barely hide his tired face, his disenchantment.

I offered him my hand, but he only pushed me away. Above us the islanders watched, beneath the green of the ash trees, the hickory strand. I strained for a smile, stayed by his side. Up above in the sky the vultures floated in slow spirals.

───────────────

When I told her it was time to leave, she brightened. 'I'll go home,' she said, 'and get my things. I can be back in an hour.' It was then I realized she believed I meant to take her with me. Preposterous, of course, but I felt no need to tell her so harshly and sought instead to disillusion her as gently as she allowed.

'I think that will be impossible, my dear,' I said. I was in front of the bathroom mirror, shaving. 'My plans are made, Nancy; my suitcases are packed. I have found nothing to keep me here.' She stood behind me, her arms round my waist, wearing one of her ugly dresses. I was tired of the soiled hotel wallpaper, the grimy bathroom, of perpetually feeling squalid and besmirched and irritated with the sullen desk clerk who always hissed at my back. I was sick of a town jealous that my existence was not, like theirs, confined to a few miles of dreary fields in the middle of a lake. 'I've made reservations on the ferry already. I am expected on the mainland at a precise hour. My train ticket is purchased. Do you even have any funds with which to purchase your own?'

Her arms dropped from my waist. 'I could pay you back.'

'Yes, perhaps you could, but my reasoning is not purely financial. I live in a bachelor apartment, Nancy. There's barely room for myself there, let alone to keep a girl. And I'm always travelling. Really, it's an intolerable life. I am being merciful, sparing you from sharing in it.'

'I could help you with your research, like I did here,' she said.

I sat on the edge of the bed, adjusting my cufflinks. 'You kept me company, Nancy, and for that I do thank you. You must agree, though, that it's a bit of a stretch to say you helped conduct any actual research.' *Any more than my shadow aided me*, I thought, for that was what she was, a shade always tagging at my heel, although naturally I did not say that.

'If I can't come, maybe you could stay,' she said. 'A little while longer, anyway? You said you were hoping to meet my father. And you said we might take a trip to Ohio and look into the sightings that were reported there.'

'I depart tomorrow night. I don't think the Canadian Pacific Railway would obligingly refund my ticket.' I knew it would do no good to foster sentiment. She had excelled at her purpose; she had been the means with which to relieve my accumulating frustrations on this island. Imagining her as anything more than that would be a disservice to the both of us. I would not play host to such unrealities.

'So you're leaving,' she said. She was crouching low by the bed, her face in her hands. It seemed such an animal position.

'Nancy, really, you needn't look so *stricken*. Listen,' I said, 'I should think you'd be well accustomed to this sort of thing by now.' She climbed onto the bed beside me, pressing her face so fiercely against my chest I felt her teeth mark the skin beneath my shirt. Wincing, I stroked her hair again in an attempt at consolation. I licked my lips; I tasted the salt of my blood. I had pursued her, it was true, but it had been a mistake, evidently for both of us, and I was not about to squander the cosmic potential of my existence on the bleak rocks of this island.

Nancy got to her feet slowly, her hands smoothing out her skirt, and it seemed a sort of calmness had settled over her as she wandered through the room, picking up her things. Her slip, her scarf, her coral crochet purse with the Bakelite handle shaped like a yellow peacock.

'Good girl,' I said. 'You understand. I knew you would.'

'*Good girl* is what you call a dog when it does what you tell it to,' she said. 'I hate it.' I chose to ignore her. She took a clock down from the mantel, the glass etched with an impression of ships. '*Tempus fugit.* That's Latin, isn't it? Don't you speak it?'

'I don't speak it, Nancy. Who would I converse with? It's a dead language. I can read and understand it, however.'

'So what does it mean?' she asked, gazing at me.

'Time flies.' But I could as easily have said it meant *love conquers* and she never would have known. Actually, the more accurate translation was, in fact, *time flees*, but such precision would be wasted on her.

'Thank you,' she said as she put the clock back. 'I always wondered.'

I said, 'We should take one last walk together.' It was the evening of DeWitt West's departure. As long as he was at the docks waiting for the ferry no later than seven, he said, he could see no harm in it.

'Where should we walk?'

'Wherever you want to go.'

He left his fine luggage at the hotel, and we made our way down the dirt road. There was no one around.

'What a beautiful dusk,' I said. I wanted to run, but I knew that DeWitt West would not appreciate anything more violent than a brisk walk. His body was meticulous in every way. The sun was sinking below Lake Erie, bleeding light into the water. 'It's a sin to waste a night as beautiful as this.'

'The eye of the beholder, I suppose.'

Veils of mist clung to the trees, obscuring their leaves. The fields turned to gold by the liquefied sun. Across the road from the docks, a pair of mourning doves cooed along the telephone wires, asking *who, who, who,* haunting and low.

'Where should we go now?'

'Why don't you decide, Nancy? The direction is of no consequence to me. Here it is all the same.'

'How about that pathway up through the forest, the one that leads along the lake?'

'All right,' he agreed.

I smiled at him, wide enough to show my teeth. 'But you might ruin your lovely clothes.'

'I'll have to throw half my belongings away, anyway, after I leave. That filthy hotel is infested with insects.'

I followed him up the grey abandoned trail. Each time he cut through a spinier thicket, the branches lashed backwards. He never bothered holding back the brush for me. The trees arced above us. I sought his hand. He brushed mine away, as if it were a blackfly droning too close. Where there were gaps in the forest shrouding us, the lake gleamed through. It shone smooth as a mirror, barely a ripple. Not even a gull disturbed the surface.

'Look,' I said. 'There's something in the lake.'

His entire body stiffened. 'What is it?'

'Something disappearing below the waves and then—it's slithering up again.'

'Where, Nancy?'

'Between the trees,' I said. 'Out over those rocks. If we turn around now we can make it to the beach—'

'The view's better up here, anyway.'

'DeWitt,' I said, 'be careful. Don't go too close to the edge.'

He turned back towards me for a moment. His eyes said he knew better. Then he disappeared through the glistening green of the trees. He didn't listen to me.

I knew he wouldn't. He wore that same indulgent smile whenever I spoke.

It was probably still on his lips as he began to fall, that grin—unbroken, confident, assuming. DeWitt West would not be thwarted. There was a rush of dirt yielding, crumbling, and muffled somewhere in there, DeWitt West's shout as he plunged towards the rocks.

When I made my way back down the grey path and stood on the road overlooking the lake, I saw him again. He lay twenty feet below, black and crooked, lodged in the rocks. Curiously, the waves lapped up around his body, caressing him, then drawing away. And then, obligingly, the lake opened its arms and carried him off.

They found him seven days later. A late summer storm dragged his body up on the beach. His photograph in the local paper, grainy and grey. *DeWitt West, amateur naturalist*. The lake had robbed him of his dark hat, his gold watch, his pince-nez. A tragic accident, the paper called it. They never found out what it was.

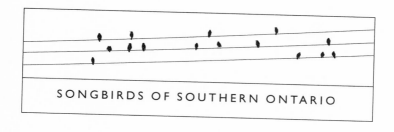

SONGBIRDS OF SOUTHERN ONTARIO

When I try to explain the things that get me down, they sound weird. But they get me down. Really down. To the point I start thinking about pills. Even though I did take pills before. *Take two capsules every morning for nerves,* the bottle said. Which seemed quaint, as if they were smelling salts. The pills never worked for me. By that I mean they didn't make me happy. Instead they made me grind my teeth, and I couldn't sleep at night, which left me even more time to think about all the things I didn't want to.

So for now I just let weird things bring me down. Things like children's books that aren't even supposed to be sad, or those animal hats with whiskers and ears hanging down, or the coffee cup we used to have, a novelty relic from the eighties with a man in oversized sunglasses and six or seven leis and on the side it said, *Happy birthday to a wild and crazy guy!* The cup bothered me so much that every time I pulled it out of the cupboard I felt like I was setting myself up to have a bad day. Finally I got rid of it, in a box I dropped off at the community thrift store, along with books I'd read and hadn't liked and some baby things because we agreed Ella was our last baby, Aidan vehemently and me reluctantly. At the last minute I pulled out a skull-print bra from the box even though it didn't really fit me anymore, but it was one of the last things I bought from Zellers before they closed their doors forever. Am I overly sentimental? Also because when I wore it, I felt a little like a rock star, like this could be the start of becoming the girl I felt I had been meant to be—a girl with pink hair and great tattoos and one of those beautiful rhinestone piercings stuck through the cheek—instead of who I really was.

I was wearing my skull-print bra that day when I got back from the dentist. I was in a pretty good mood because the dentist had told me he could see I took very good care of my teeth. I wasn't sure if that was true, because I drank a lot of coffee and usually fell asleep with one of the kids before I could brush them at night, but it had made me happy, anyway. When I walked in the door, though, Aidan was waiting in the kitchen with Ella sleeping in his arms.

'She cried the whole time you were gone,' he said, and he was vaguely accusatory about it, like I'd willed her to do it, as if I could manage her emotions by remote control. I could hear Ruby and Harlow in the living room, taking turns jumping off the coffee table. They thought if they did this enough times they would eventually learn to fly. *You can't fly*, Aidan said, *you're not birds*, but I remained noncommittal. *Maybe you will*, I told them, *one day*.

'I'm sorry,' I said, running my tongue across my clean teeth.

Aidan shrugged. 'The mattress broke.'

'Why?'

'It just did.'

'But what's the reason?'

'Sometimes there is no reason,' he said.

I said, 'There always is a reason. Only sometimes we don't know it.'

'Just come see.' And I followed him down the hall. He flipped the lights on in our bedroom and I saw what he meant, one side of the mattress sagging almost to the floor. 'Did you get the warranty?'

'No,' I said. 'I don't believe in warranties.'

Aidan rolled his eyes and handed me Ella. 'You're a mother now, Venera,' he said. 'You need to think about these things.'

'It's my side of the bed anyway,' I said, 'so what do you care?' I hated when he reminded me I was a mother. As if it was something he thought I could ever forget.

When Ruby was three and Harlow was a year and I was pregnant with Ella, I brought the girls to the market on Ottawa Street. It was wintertime and we were mostly stuck in the house, so once a week we would go to smell the handmade soaps and look at old coins and peruse the stand that sold minerals and crystals. We'd buy some fruit or maybe something sprouting and green, like arugula or wheatgrass, which I usually ended up letting wilt away on my windowsill. I pushed Ruby in a stroller and wore Harlow strapped to my chest, where she sucked on handfuls of my hair as my fingers swam for change in the swamp of my purse. 'You know what they say,' said the woman at the deli counter. 'One is one and two is twenty.' My coat was stashed under the stroller and when I crouched to check the pockets for loose coins, Harlow grabbed hold of Ruby's hair. 'Mama she's hurting me,' Ruby shrieked. I tried to unknot Harlow's fingers but she'd locked her little hands like a pit bull clamps his jaw. Ruby was starting up the grumbled whine she did, what Aidan called the Ruby chainsaw. I pushed a cookie in the direction of her mouth. 'Look at you,' the deli woman said, 'super mom.' 'Thank you,' I said, and I smiled, but only when I walked away did I figure out the deli woman hadn't been sincere. I felt deflated and stupid, like when you think you've been having this really glamorous and beautiful moment and realize after the fact you had lipstick on your teeth the whole time.

Remember, you have three beautiful girls.

It was the last thing Aidan's mother said to me after we dropped off the girls, as we stood in the doorway. She whispered it in my ear, holding Ella in her arms as she leaned in to say goodbye. I knew it was her way of saying we had better find a way to make this work. That was why she was sending us to Pelee Island for the weekend while she watched the girls. To relax, she said. But she had other motives. The preservation of our marriage, mainly.

'Your mother thinks we're going to get divorced,' I said as I pulled out of the driveway.

'That's ridiculous,' Aidan said. 'Keep your phone charged this weekend. You never know when we're going to get a call from my parents saying Ruby broke her arm trying to fly.'

'She won't break her arm.'

'You need to tell the girls they can't fly,' Aidan said. 'You keep lying to them about it.'

'I'm not lying to them,' I said. 'I just don't want to take away their hope.'

'That's the same as lying,' Aidan said, and I said, 'No, it isn't. I don't want to crush their creative spirits.'

'That's some hippie bullshit,' he said.

We drove without talking the rest of the way. Aidan listened to 'Ava Adore' over and over. I looked out the window, at the green sweep of fields and dark woodlots and thought about the girls. I was missing them already. It made me sad that we wouldn't read *The Star Money* together before bed, even though usually I sighed when Ruby chose that book night after night. It was a fairy tale about an orphan girl who gives away everything she has—her bread, her clothes, her little hat. And then the stars take pity on her and start falling down around her, becoming silver coins. Ruby loved the picture of the girl holding up her skirt in the middle of the woods at night, catching the dropping stars, but the story unsettled me. *There was once upon a time a little girl whose father and mother were dead.* Did Ruby understand it? Did she care? I wondered if she might be sociopathic. I remembered learning, in a psychology class I'd taken at university, that one of the signs was a weak startle reflex. When we got back I would test it, somehow. Jump out of a closet, or from behind a door. Then I'd have to measure her blinks or her heartbeat. I would look it up.

On the ferry, we went up on deck. Aidan got seasick while I leaned over the railing. I always secretly hoped I might catch a glimpse of a sea serpent, and though I recognized on a rational level this was absurd, you could never know anything for sure. So I stood there, gazing down at the grey-green water, waiting for a scaled coil or hump to break the surface. I thought again about our daughters, and hoped Ella would be okay without me. I realized she probably would be just fine, which relieved me, but which also felt like a little bit of a letdown because it made me think about how easily we can all be replaced. Even monkeys, in that terrible science experiment, learned to love warm towels wrapped around a bottle of milk. Still, I decided to send good thoughts to the girls.

I wondered if we did share a secret mother-daughter bond, some sort of telepathy or wavelength. If I had that with any of my daughters it would be Ella, I reasoned, since we had shared the experience of an emergency C-section together. It must have been pretty traumatic for her. I imagined Ella, curled up and bobbing in the water of my womb, sleeping even, maybe, when suddenly the sky of my stomach opened up. The blinding light, the doctor's gloved hands tugging her up towards it. It would probably be a lot like the experience of people who claimed aliens had abducted them, that sudden snatching from above, the medical prodding, and I felt a new rush of sympathy for them, although Aidan always maintained it was impossible. But I felt it was unwise to rule any-thing out.

On the deck I closed my eyes and concentrated on telegraph-ing a calm feeling of love to all three of the girls. I focused on Ella. I told her to be happy, and that she would be okay when she cried in the middle of the night, even if I wasn't there.

———————

At the bed and breakfast on West Shore Road, Evie, our hostess, had arranged a little library on our bed. *Songbirds of Southern Ontario,* a neatly folded map, and a bicycle guide to the island. It seemed so hopeful and sweet. I flipped through the pages of the bicycle guide. We might visit the glacial grooves or the cemetery, it suggested, or the stone lighthouse built at the edge of a marsh.

Aidan said, 'I can't sleep in this room. The wallpaper is giving me anxiety.'

'What's wrong with it?' I asked. It was cream coloured, with fading vines and blackberries.

'All those little berries clustered together,' he said.

I looked at the wallpaper again. The blackberries *were* pretty clumped together, constellations of tiny dark holes. I knew Aidan had a problem with things like that—ants swarming the crack on a sidewalk, bunches of mushrooms sprouting in damp grass, the holes on a lotus seed head. 'Well, what can we do?'

'Ask for another room.'

'I don't want to bother our hostess.'

'I have trypophobia,' he said.

'Right,' I said, 'I know, but Evie already told us all the rooms are booked.'

'What am I supposed to do?' Aidan asked.

And I said, 'close your eyes.'

Afterwards as we lay in bed, side by side and silent, I felt like I hadn't been very supportive, so I reached over and tried patting his shoulder in what I hoped was a comforting way.

'It's okay,' I said. 'I'm sorry. I know you have a phobia, I understand. It's reflexive.'

'Venera, we've had a long day, let's go to sleep.'

So we did.

In the morning I called Aidan's mother to check on the girls.

'They're fine,' she said.

'Really?'

'Venera, I raised four children of my own,' she said. 'I think I know what I'm doing.'

'Oh I know, I know,' I said quickly. 'Just, you know, we're not used to being apart at night—'

'They slept just fine,' she cut in. 'They didn't ask for you once.'

'Great,' I said. And I meant it, of course, but still. I told myself my telepathy had worked, that they had sensed my love from across the lake, had been comforted by it, and hadn't needed to ask.

'Venera,' she said, 'go and have a good time. Rent bicycles. Go to the beach. The weather's supposed to be perfect today.'

We said goodbye, and I hung up the phone. Across the room, Aidan flicked off the television contemptuously.

'The only thing coming in clearly is weather reports from Ohio,' he said.

'I don't think we're supposed to watch TV here.'

'Then what are we supposed to do?'

I looked out the window. 'Enjoy nature, I guess.'

'Yeah,' he said. 'No thanks. I've had enough nature. I'm covered in mosquito bites from ten minutes sitting in the gazebo last night. And it's supposed to be like ninety degrees today. Why the hell did my mother send us to this penal colony?'

'Well,' I said. 'It's already nine o'clock. If we don't go downstairs now, we'll miss breakfast.'

To my relief, the dining room décor was free of clusters. The wallpaper was cream with white feathers drifting across. Evie and a guest were discussing making their own jam with sugar, strawberries, and lemon juice. 'You have to bring the water to a roiling boil,' Evie said, and the guest said, 'See, that's where I go wrong. I think I've just been bringing the water to a simmer.'

'Oh, no,' Evie murmured, shaking her head, as if the woman had confessed a mild sin, like shoplifting for pleasure. I sat down across from Aidan.

'Good morning,' Evie said, after the guest had finished

troubleshooting her jam-making process and disappeared outside. 'You slept well, I hope?'

'Oh, yes.'

'Do you have any plans today?' Evie asked.

'No,' I admitted, 'not really. Not yet.'

Evie smiled. Her pink dress matched the pale flowers on the teacups and dishes—bone china saucers trimmed in gold, which I felt neither Aidan nor I appreciated as much as we should. Peonies, I thought, and everything had a little scalloped edge. For years I'd thought bone china meant white, like bones, but from my own mother I'd recently learned it was because there was actually bone ash from animals in it. It seemed like a grotesque and unnecessary touch, and also not okay for vegetarians. My mother said it was about chip resistance.

Evie said, 'Perhaps you'd be interested in one of the nature reserves. I left some maps in your room, and a book about the birds you might see. It's May, so the indigo buntings have just arrived. Have you ever seen them? They're just beautiful.'

'What are they?' Aidan asked.

Evie blinked, like she was a little shocked by Aidan's ignorance. 'Songbirds,' she said. 'Of course, only the breeding males are that stunning blue. The females are mostly brown, although sometimes there can be a bit of blue to their wings.'

'We'll definitely have to keep our eyes open,' I said.

Evie smiled, but not like she smiled at the guest who'd botched her jams. 'Well. What can I get you to drink?'

'Do you have any Red Bull?' Aidan asked.

'No, I'm afraid not. We have coffee, and orange juice we make ourselves here—'

'The juice sounds wonderful,' I said, desperate to compensate for our obvious deficiencies. 'Can we have that, please? Thanks so much.' For some reason I was a big sucker for the approval of older women. I could see we were not the sort of couple Evie had set up this place for, and I felt her quiet disappointment, subtly, like the way you could feel the displacement of air by a songbird's blue wing.

'I thought maybe they were butterflies or something,' Aidan said. 'Or some uncommon wildflower, I don't know.'

I shrugged. We stopped at the first beach we found. I kept thinking of my pills, how maybe I should have brought them even though they didn't work that way, a quick fix. You had to take them every day, let them sort of accumulate inside. 'Do you even like spending time with me?'

Aidan sighed. 'Of course I do, Venera, what do you think this is? Community-service hours?'

'You called it a penal colony.'

Last week I brought our cat, Olive, to the veterinarian. I hadn't wanted to leave after the appointment was over. I kept asking the vet questions so he wouldn't stop talking to me. I even acted out this scenario like we were planning on getting a puppy. 'So what would you say is the healthiest breed? And how early is too early for the puppies to leave their mother?'

'Oh, eight weeks or so and you're good,' he'd said.

'Really, now. Because that sounds just so young—'

'Well, a dog's done nursing at seven, eight weeks. They're not like cats. I've seen cats nursing kittens from the previous litter as they're giving birth to the next batch.'

I'd glanced at Olive with new appreciation. I'd had no idea she was so maternal.

'Well,' the vet said, 'it was nice chatting with you. I have a dog with a pretty bad ear infection waiting for me, so....' I stared at the poster about the facts of dog dental care for about five minutes after he left. In the car on the way home, I suddenly started crying at a red light.

———————————

'Look, we're here,' Aidan said. 'Let's just try and have a good time.'

I wished that we didn't have to try so hard to have a good time, that it could be like it used to be, and we could just have a good time when we were together. Like the day we bought guitars at the pawnshop and tried to teach ourselves to play 'Glycerine', or the way we used to walk by the river, holding hands, the water lit by the cool metal gleam of Detroit's skyline. I thought about the first summer we were together. We'd rented a cottage on the lake, spent the afternoons filling mason jars with beach glass. I got to my feet, hiked my sundress up over my knees, waded into the water, leaving Aidan on the shore. My feet sank in the slosh of seaweed, oily green on my ankles. Little fish, flickering silver, flitted away, slivers of light. My skirt sucked up water. I watched my dress float around my thighs, thought of the dreamy pre-Raphaelite paintings of Ophelia. In the portrait by Millais, she wasn't searching through the trees, straining for the sky or the branch forever just out of reach. She wasn't absorbed in morbid make-believe beside a lily pond, decorating her long hair with petals and leaves, rosemary for remembrance, *pray you, love, remember*. She just drifted in the river on her back, palms up, lips parted. Strands of flowers dripped between her cold fingers, garnishing her wet pale bodice.

Aidan was calling from the beach. 'Venera, come back. You're going too far.' I took a breath, went under, surfaced closer to the shore. Aidan waded out to his knees. 'You don't know where it drops off.'

I closed my eyes and felt the warmth of the sunlight caress my face. In some places on the island, the water was so clean and clear you could see down to the bottom, to the sparkle of pebbles and shells, to the hard glitter of sand in the sun below the waves. Here the lake was murky, a dark sludge of seaweed and dead silt always churning up, cloudy and cold. Zebra mussels, with their little striped shells, shattered over the beach and under your feet when you swam. They were an invasive species let loose in the ballast water of ships returning from the ocean in the Saint Lawrence Seaway. They crusted the beach, and they broke sharp enough to cut your feet, let your blood unspool red into the water.

I thought about Aidan after our first date when we were nineteen and walking home in the snow, about how we'd kissed, the damp wool of my mittens on his face. It had been the most romantic moment of my life, even though we were standing in an alley behind the adult video store. I thought of him during the C-section, when they were tunnelling in through my lower abdomen to excavate Ella, about how he'd stood there and pressed his forehead to mine saying, *Venera, I love you. I love you so much*, pressing so hard it hurt, but how reassuring it was to feel him there, when the rest of my body was so numb.

I drew my legs up, floated, dipped below the surface again, held my breath till I heard Aidan calling me back. Just to hear him say my name with feeling and mean it. I surfaced with water in my eyes and ears, bereft of breath, the blood throb of my heart beating in my throat. I wondered if this was how it was now, having to go out farther and farther, wretched and reckless, to try to restart my sputtering heart. I would go back, I decided, to Aidan, to the shore.

And when I got back to Evie, I would tell her we had gone to the nature reserve after all. I would tell her that we'd seen the indigo buntings, and that they were the most beautiful birds we'd ever witnessed.

OH HOW WE MISS YOU.
HOW ABOUT JOINING US?

Here's the thing: we are not allowed to turn the lights on. Creed says it costs fifteen cents every time you touch a switch. 'Waste not, want not,' he murmurs, burying onion bulbs in jars of dirt along the kitchen windowsill. He regrows celery this way, too, in small saucers of water, and lettuce. He has an avocado pit he hopes will one day become a tree.

We are not allowed to turn the lights on, no matter how dark the night might get. Creed says we can retrain our eyes like this. We will see as cats do, sensitive and sharp, feeling our way, intuitive. He says that seeing in the dark is a lost art, like blacksmithing or making candles from beeswax. You can get used to anything, he says.

I nod, looking at the glass jars all along the windowsill, the ones brimming with new green, and all his empty jars, too—the star-jelly ones. Jealous, I watch him gather all the little pieces of onions and leeks, the cuttings pressed so tenderly into the earth, feeling the hope in his hands as he wills them to be alive.

The summer Danny went missing was the same summer the star jelly appeared out of nowhere. In the mornings you would see it quivering in the grass or clinging to tree branches, translucent and mucous-like. Millie said it was algae from the lake, or toad spawn. 'No,' August said. She crouched in the long grass under the hickory trees, the clear pulpish thing cupped in her hands, trembling. 'It's from the stars. That's what Creed says.'

Maybe airplanes were the source of star jelly. Some mix of weather, coolant from a leak in the air-conditioning system, somehow gelatinizing on its way down to earth before plopping to the grass. But when I said that to Creed, he shook his head. He sat at the kitchen table, gazing out the window, tattooed knuckles wrapped around his teacup. He drank black tea in the mornings, lemon balm in the evenings. I would see him in the garden in the afternoon, hands full of rosehips and lavender, sun shining on his back.

'You don't got no faith, Angel.'

But what he meant was that I believed in the wrong things. Like how I believed Danny would come back to me, somehow, even after he'd been gone a month.

'I have a question for you,' Danny said the night we met. White Nirvana t-shirt, restless hands dipping in and out of the pockets of his jeans. 'About my car. You're a mechanic? I have this, like, snapping noise in my dashboard when I start it.'

'Sounds like it could be your HVAC door actuators.'

'What?'

'They change the settings for the heating and cooling system. But your noise could be something else. I'd have to take a look at the car to know. Pinpoint where in the dash the sound is coming from. Bring it to my place Monday, if you want.'

'Yeah,' he said, nodding. For a moment his hands stopped moving. 'Maybe I should give that a try.'

'You're better than Ativan for me,' Danny used to say, and for a while it felt good to believe it. But as our months together turned into a year, it felt less a compliment and more an omen. Mornings he would stay in bed. Sometimes when I came home at five he would still be there with the television on, and other times he would be asleep again. Or he'd never woken up in the first place.

'Didn't you have work today?'

'I called in sick,' he'd say, if he did answer.

Here's the things I wanted to remember: The way his eyes shut when he really laughed. How on good afternoons we went to Sandpoint Beach. The weekends we stayed up all night watching *Teenage Mutant Ninja Turtles*. I wanted to remember the soap he bought me, the one with crushed walnut shells to scour away grease and cocoa butter for when I burned myself on an exhaust, the way he smoothed it into my raw skin until it healed. The way he would say, 'Angel, you missed a spot,' when he found smudges of oil on the backs of my arms. Like being in love with the Tin Man, Danny would say, lifting the hem of his shirt to wipe it all away.

———————————

It was dark when Danny and I arrived at the farmhouse just outside of town. It was the kind of small Ontario town where people wore camouflage even when they weren't going hunting. They had grown up here, Danny and Creed, before Creed changed his name.

'What was his name before?'

'What do you care?' he said, but then he answered. 'It's Ciro. "Of the sun."'

Behind the house was Lake Erie. Walk under the cedars, the blue ash, and you would come to a limestone outcrop above the lake. There used to be a beach here, Danny told me, as we stood over the water. But it was gone now.

'All right. We better go inside. Don't turn the lights on if you don't have to. It's a rule of Creed's.'

The door was unlocked. I held Danny's hand, tried to see through the shadows. A wood-panelled room, bleary photographs of the lake in crooked frames, yellow stacks of damp *National Geographics* everywhere. A pair of ducks, nailed to the wall, wings arranged in a stiff imitation of flight. Their glass-bead eyes blinked when a car's headlights cut through the room. As the beam of light moved, I noticed a loveseat underneath the birds. Two people sat there, a third on the floor — a girl with long hair being woven into a fishtail braid by the girl above her.

'Nice to meet you,' the man said. 'I'm Creed.' A silver ring pierced his septum. On his neck were tattooed the phases of the moon. Sitting to his right, braiding, a girl in a pair of satin leopard-print pyjama shorts fringed with dark lace, her tattooed thighs visible below. Her bare legs were tucked up to the side, ending in slippers, puffs of pale pink fur. Her eyeliner was shiny and black as an oil leak.

'Millie.'

'August,' said the other.

'Do you got anything to drink?' Danny asked.

'Nothing you'd want.' I felt Creed's eyes as they went to my stomach, briefly, though in Danny's Megadeth shirt there was not much to see yet, just the album cover for *Killing Is My Business*. 'I can make you some tea. Lemon balm. Raspberry leaf, if you're past your first trimester.'

'I'm not.'

'It's late,' Danny said.

'Let me say some words, at least. As your brother. To celebrate your new marriage.'

Danny sighed. 'If you have to.'

Creed rose. 'It's the right thing to do.'

'And you always do the right thing,' Danny said. 'Right?'

('What came first,' my mother said when we told her we were getting married, 'the engagement or the baby?'

'Does it matter?' I asked.

'It used to,' she said. 'But nothing matters anymore, I guess.')

In each of his hands, Creed took one of ours. Danny tensed but let him. He was still wearing his aviators, and I wondered if he could see at all. Creed's knuckles and fingers were tattooed down to his palms. Nautical stars and anchors, thin black scalloped lines like waves. Scales on the backs of his hands.

'May the most you wish for be the least you get,' he said.

Danny stood there silently. The girls stared.

'Thank you,' I said. My gumball-machine ring, a tiny gold claw holding a round blue stone, felt tight around my finger.

Creed smiled. 'I always wanted a sister.'

———————

Sitting in our bed, I watched Danny blunder with the lock. 'Which one is your brother's girlfriend?'

'I don't get involved,' he said, not turning around, 'and neither should you.'

'Can't you just turn the light on? For a second?'

And he said, 'You don't understand his rules, but I know the way he is.'

It was cold upstairs, in our new room, that rainy June night. At one time the house had been rented to hunters, and on the wall was a handwritten sign— *Please remember we are on a septic system* in fading cursive. In the bathroom there was a similar reminder, the word *caution* underlined in faded ink. 'He seems all right.'

There was a postcard tacked to the wall, by the window. Four cartoon birds on a wire, pop-eyed, open-mouthed, tweeting away. *Oh How We Miss You*, they sang. *How About Joining Us?*

Danny shrugged. The door finally latched. He took off his t-shirt, dropped it on the damp carpet. 'You'll see,' he said. 'Sooner or later.'

———————

Danny said Millie and August were out of their minds, the way they went out every night. 'That isn't nice,' I said, but secretly I wondered. Without fail, they gathered up their jars that, if they were lucky, they would fill with star jelly. Whatever they found always dissolved by midday, but still they seemed dutiful, permanently undeterred. Nights I couldn't sleep, I heard them coming up the stairs, in the murky hours after midnight and before the sunrise, their glass jars clinking, their low whispers disappearing behind the other bedroom door.

'They just pick that shit up with their bare hands,' Danny said. 'Toxic slime from some factory, probably. You can see the nuclear power stations in Ohio from here if you look across the lake.'

Millie said, 'There have always been things that fall from the sky.' She spoke of showers of fish, frogs, starfish, and crabs, heaven's mysterious gifts. A hail of peaches over Louisiana. Navy beans on the night of March 6th, 1958, in Van Nuys, California. A cloudburst of hazelnuts over Bristol, England, 1977. Silver coins raining down in a yucca garden in Jalisco. Paper money in the streets of Limburg, West Germany, 1977. A shiny black rock of unknown origin shattering on a patio in Toronto in 1978, leaving even geologists at the Royal Ontario Museum baffled. So this jelly was only one of thousands of unexpected objects that dropped from the clouds or the heavens above. It was believed to have been the remains of shooting stars, maybe meteors — *pwdre ser*, rot of the stars. Sometimes it was called angel hair.

I didn't look up from what I was doing, slipping an elastic band around the button of my jeans. Makeshift maternity clothes. 'What are they going to do with it?'

'That's not the point.'

They asked me, sometimes, if I would join them.

'Don't even think about it,' Danny said.

———

It was Creed who taught Danny, when they were teenagers, how to throw a punch: hard with your knuckles, thumb tucked tight so you didn't break your own bones. At my shop's New Year's Eve party, Danny's form had been flawless, and all his bones were fine afterwards, even though he had to ice his hand in the snow crusting the parking lot of the Croatian Centre as I stood frozen in my green satin dress, slush seeping into my salt-stained high heels. But Graziano, my boss, swinging back for Danny's jaw, had broken his own ring finger. Which was why we were here, cramped in a bunk bed in Danny's childhood bedroom still with the Garfield sheets, hockey cards in the drawers. It was close to the seafood restaurant in town where Danny's friend had got him a job washing dishes, a place we could live without paying rent.

'As long as you want,' Creed offered. He was crushing tea leaves at the kitchen table. Millie worked by his side, her headband holding all her hair back in a voluminous dark bun. First he had steamed the leaves, then let them dry on baking sheets. I had been watching him all morning as I turned the musty pages of a *National Geographic* from the seventies reading an article about oarfish, mysterious deep-sea creatures so often mistaken for monsters.

'Just until we get back on our feet,' Danny said.

'You're always welcome in my house.'

'I don't want to be here.'

Creed said, 'Well. But it looks like you got nowhere else to go.'

Because this house had been rented to hunters and there was death in every room, Danny said. A blood smell, even with the windows open.

Chewing on a white tea leaf, Millie got to her feet. 'Come on, Angel,' she said. 'August is picking chamomile. You coming, or what?'

————————

'It's like all day I've got the same sad radio station playing in my head,' Danny said, finishing the whisky in his glass. 'And sometimes at the end of the day I have to press mute.'

'Why can't you just change the station?' I asked. Over us, in the dark wooden slats of the bunk above, was a compendium of diverse obscenities cut by Danny's teenage hand.

'It doesn't work that way.'

On the windowsill, he left the glass—Ziggy in a yellow sweater, hands clasped under the caption, *Hi … it's nice to have you here.* ('That was your favourite when we were kids,' Creed said. 'You always had to have your juice in it.' And Danny said, 'I don't remember.')

'Maybe I could help you,' I said, but he didn't answer. My heartburn made it hard to swallow. You couldn't hold on to Danny anymore; he had become thin and prickly as the milk thistle that grew in the roadside ditches here. His eyes were closed, one hand open over his chest, the other busy with his ritualized stroke, fingers passing over the pocket of his jeans. This was the night before he disappeared. Earlier that day he had bought a TV at the St. Vincent de Paul thrift store downtown. We watched *Teenage Mutant Ninja Turtles*. There was no moon that night, so our only light was what the television gave. I tried reading a *National Geographic*, tilting the pages towards the glow of the screen, before giving up.

'Why can't we turn the lights on?'

Danny rose up on one elbow, glanced over me towards the closed door, as if there was someone on the other side.

'Why even have electricity at all?' I threw the magazine down on the carpet. (August had explained it. 'We're subordinate to technology, Creed says. Living unnatural lives, estranged from the natural world.')

'He's just flexing his muscles,' Danny said. 'Seeing what he can do. What we'll let him do.'

'He says there's so much light pollution at night, no one can see the stars anymore,' I said. 'That most of us don't even know the night sky.'

'So stick some plastic glow-in-the-dark stars on your ceiling, then.'

But it was true: I never really saw stars till I came out here. The sky over the city was murky, smirched with fluorescence. Here you could see the real night sky. On TV was the *Ninja Turtles* episode where Kraang created humanoid frogs in a subterranean laboratory. Danny lay back down, closed his eyes again. I liked to think, afterwards, that if I had known it was the last time I would see Danny, I would have tried to make it different, better, more meaningful. But the sad thing is, maybe I wouldn't have done anything differently at all.

'I have to go to the bathroom. I'm tired of banging into things at night. You should see the bruises—'

'Get a candle,' Danny said. 'Or just turn the lights on. I'm sick of being here.' And before I knew what he was doing, he reached out, flipped the switch on the wall beside the bed. The lightbulb flickered, then held a steady glow. The inside of the bulb was speckled darkly with dead flies.

———————————

Mornings were when we went to the garden to get what we needed for the day. Creed and the girls sold tea at farmers' markets and local restaurants. Their creative blends were inspired by the Carolinian forests of southern Ontario. Nettles, wild mint, maple blossoms. Creed led tours where he taught about foraging, bringing groups through the woods looking for mushrooms, purslane, and chickweed.

In the garden, August showed me the scar from her Caesarean, lifting up her dress. 'But that won't happen to you, Angel,' she said. 'I'm sure you'll have a natural birth.' She gazed at me. 'Creed was asking about you. You should talk to him. He can help you, you know.'

'Help me with what?'

'Whatever you need,' she said.

The morning before I had gone into town, to Lakeshore Quick Lube & Vehicle Repair, my resumé in a file folder. No reference from Graziano—not after what happened at the party—but still,

I came from one of the best shops. The place other shops sent work to. But the manager had taken one look at the hump of my stomach popping the buttons of my last good shirt and thanked me. Said they weren't hiring now but maybe later, and I knew it didn't matter what kind of shop I came from, or that they used to say I could beat the times in the labour guide, I was that fast and that good. None of it mattered anymore, not even in this dirty place with banners blazing in the windows advertising cheap safeties. It wasn't a good time. I didn't have to go back into Windsor to see the sign on the side of the Lion's Head, *GOD SAVE THE BIG THREE*, or the bumper stickers asking, *Hungry Yet? Eat Your Foreign Car*, to see my hopes for employment receding like the tide.

'I don't need anything,' I said.

'I wish you wouldn't keep your heart so closed to him.' August knelt with her knife to cut a few sprigs of lemon balm, the leaves just starting to yellow. 'He can help you, you know, in ways even doctors can't, with their needles and drugs. It's in the way he looks at you, shining with love.'

———————

Here's the thing: it is easier in some ways to be here now that Danny is gone. And the absence of guilt can become its own kind of guilt. The second night, Millie knocked on my door and, without waiting for an answer, came inside.

'You shouldn't be alone.' Hair heaped in a shiny black bump, angled eyeliner, like one of the Ronettes. Ronnie singing 'Be My Baby' in her white high heels. *Oh how we miss you.* Millie climbed into bed. *How about joining us?* 'Unless you want to be?'

(The day before, Danny had woken me as he left for work, a thing he never did. Laid a hand on my back. 'Angel,' he said. 'The car won't start. I think the battery's dead. I'll walk to work.'

I didn't even lift my face from the pillow. Heartburn had kept me up at night. I was barely awake. 'But I just put in a new battery.'

'I must've forgot I left the lights on or something,' he said.)

Millie's breath was steady, lulling, the way the lake was, beyond the trees, the open windows. 'No,' I said. 'I guess I'd rather not be.'

'I can stay here till midnight,' she said. 'Then I'm going out. You can join us, you know.'

I wanted her to offer to braid my hair, too, the way she had August's that first night, but she didn't. 'Maybe another time.'

She pointed at the curse words sliced into the slats of the bunk. *Fuck you whoever sees this* carved so deep into the wood you wondered at the fury in the hand that held the knife. 'You should change that. It's bad energy to have above you every night.'

In the morning, I climbed into the car, still parked where Danny had left it in the gravel driveway. In the quiet dark encircling the farmhouse, you would have noticed the harshness of headlights cutting through the trees. The car grumbled to life, in need of an oil change, but the battery was fine. Only a week earlier I'd changed it.

Afterwards I went down to the lake, the day slick with sunshine. Before I got to the water there was Creed, by the edge of the trees. The sunlight shone over him, wavering gold through the leaves. His hands were full of wild leeks, a row laid across a white tea towel spread over the dirt.

'The first rule of foraging,' he said, 'is that you never take the entire plant. You never take more than you need.' He was close enough I could smell the tang of raw onion on his hands. We weren't far from the farmhouse, and when I looked up, I thought for a moment that I saw movement in our bedroom window, but it must have been the sun, shining on the glass. Creed snapped a piece of leek, offered it.

'How do you eat it?'

'Just like this.' The blue on the bellflowers. Scales on the backs of his hands. Sunlight everywhere, and for a moment the world was on mute. The two of us under the ash trees. If that was Danny at the window.... But it wasn't, it was only the light.

I have no heart, the Tin Man says in the book. *And so I must be very careful.*

_____

Millie said if I told her the time and place of my birth, she could determine my rising sign, which was crucial to truly understanding yourself. She was a Pisces rising, she said, connected to all existence, which was heavy but beautiful, too.

'I only know the place,' I said. We sat on the wooden porch after the rain; the trees were eerie yellow, the clouds dark. 'I don't know the time.'

'You're an Aquarius, I bet,' Millie said. 'You have that aura all around you.'

August picked up an ash leaf, let the drops of rain drip off into her pale open hand. 'Ask your mother and we'll figure it out. She never told you?'

In the hickory trees were the wind chimes they had made, from flea market silverware and driftwood, glass beads from thrift store necklaces unstrung. 'She left me where I was born,' I said, 'in the basement washrooms at the Bay. She got freaked out, I guess. A security guard found me. They named me Antonia for Saint Anthony, patron saint of lost objects. When I was a year old, my mom went to court. She got me back and changed my name.'

'Does that mess you up for life?' August asked. Her hair, full of chamomile flowers, was gold in the light.

'She called the store. She told them where I was.'

August said, 'The basement washrooms? By the shoe department?'

'I don't know,' I said. 'I guess so.'

'I was the first baby of the year,' August said. 'They put my name in the paper. My parents won a dinner at Cadillac Jack's.'

The light dissolved over the trees. August rose, wandered off down to the lake where Creed was, even though Millie told me this was his time for meditation and he would want to be alone.

'Anyway, don't listen to August,' Millie said, her pink fur slippers off, her bare feet dragging through the wet grass. 'She's supposed to be trying to get her kid back, but she doesn't do anything about it. She doesn't know what love is. Your mother loved you. She fought for you.'

'I guess so,' I said. Above us, the sea gulls skimmed the sky. What I didn't say was that, more and more, I understood why she did what she had done, but not why she had looked back.

'Where do you think he went?' Millie asked. I was helping her ready the glass jars for the night. Each jar had a label printed first with the date, then a space left for the place the star jelly was found. The moon phases were done in ink by August, semicircles of black for tonight's waning crescent.

'I don't know,' I said, applying a label. I didn't tell them I'd called his work that morning. ('Danny hasn't been here in almost two weeks,' his manager said.) Or that his clothes had vanished from his drawers just the other day when they had been here, all this time, even after he'd gone. Hadn't they?

August said, 'Are you coming out with us tonight?'

'I don't think so. I haven't been sleeping.'

'I can make you some peppermint tea,' Millie said. 'It will help with your heartburn.'

August passed me some more labels. 'They say if you have bad heartburn, your baby will be born with a full head of hair.'

And Millie said, 'That isn't true.'

That morning, I went down to the lake, walked to where there was still some sand. Water weeds, driftwood, the glistening bodies of fish. Garbage, too—bleached and broken things, what Danny called ghost plastic. The wet dross of the world. Over the water, cumulonimbus clouds formed along the horizon of Ohio. Millie told me these clouds, made up of ice crystals, meant rain was on its way.

When I got back to the house, Creed was at the kitchen table peeling lemons. He always made us breakfast. I took the chair across from him. Lavender tea, oatmeal in a Pyrex bowl with rows of yellow dots like suns.

'I should have met you first, Angel,' he said, not looking up from the lemon. The paring knife glinted in his hands. He always got right down to the flesh. 'I wouldn't have done this to you.'

I was never the kind of mechanic who wanted to work on cars on the weekend, to restore a 1965 Thunderbird or some Cadillac from the seventies, but now I felt the urge. To diagnose and fix. *Come back, Danny*, I wanted to say. Before it was too late. The humidity already in the air. Condensation along the windowsills.

Millie said: 'One drop of water starts to form a rain cloud.'

In late summer, I got sick. So sick I slept for what felt like days and days and when I woke up it was dusk. Light like pollen scattered everywhere across the carpet and my damp sheets and Creed sitting on the edge of the bed.

'How are you feeling?'

'It's freezing in here.'

He rose and shut the open windows. 'We were waiting for your fever to break. Now that you're awake, I'll bring you some elder-flower tea.'

Outside the windows, light flickered through the trees, dark against the sky. Soon you wouldn't be able to see anything at all. When I leaned over the side of the bed and vomited, Creed held my hair back. Afterwards he washed my face.

'You've been here three months.'

'I've been here too long.'

('Do you believe in signs?' Creed asked me once, when we were alone in the kitchen as I helped him strip thyme leaves from thin green stems. A herb once thought to be a cure for melancholy, he said. Danny was still here then, and later, at night, when I'd put the same question to him, he rolled his eyes, said, 'Where's that coming from, Angel? Signs of what?' and I left it there, didn't tell him the rest of what Creed had said when I told him yes, I did believe in signs, how he smiled, murmured, 'Angel, we are so alike.')

'You can stay here for years.' Creed dipped a cloth in water, cleaned the corners of my mouth. 'But I think it's time for you to give us something. A gesture of your good faith.'

'What is that?'

'It's up to you,' he said, wringing the cloth out.

I looked back out the window, felt my fever cooling into a dewy sweat, stared at the dark sky pierced with infinite light. ('Dis-aster,' Millie said, 'comes from aster, *disastro* in Italian, ill-starred.')

Creed got up, turned to leave. 'I'd never ask for anything more than you're ready to give.'

————————————

As fall approached, I stopped trying Danny's number. The word *telephone*, Greek for 'far' and 'voice' . Once I heard Bell invented it hoping he might speak to the dead, transmit messages to phantoms over the wire.

There were prisms in all the windows of the farmhouse. Creed had found a chandelier at a yard sale and had taken it apart. On days when the sun was shining, rainbows shimmered over the floorboards, the peeling wallpaper. When I could see the rainbows, I told myself it was a good sign. September came, and the light started to go brittle. In the kitchen Creed was drying chamomile.

'You would tell me, if you knew where he was.'

'Angel, what do you think? You would be the first.'

'Where would he go?' In our bedroom Danny's Ziggy glass was still on the windowsill where he'd left it. At home he had kept the whisky in the cupboard, behind the bag of oats we never used. It made him too sad to see it out in the open, he said.

'Let's talk about how Danny isn't coming back.' Outside the windows, the pie tins rattled in the garden, strung up to ward off birds. Creed laid his paring knife down. 'When are you going to let yourself feel something more than loss?'

Oh how we miss you. We miss you. My stomach was a full moon in August's white dress. August had asked me what I was going to name the baby, but I said I was waiting to decide until Danny came back. (Before, when he was here, some days he still drank apple juice from his Ziggy cup—*it's nice to have you here*—and when he left it on the table I would lean down, check to see if it was mixed with whisky. But there were times I didn't want to know. Before he disappeared I heard him one night, talking with Creed outside, below our open window. 'If you were ever in your right mind,' Creed said, and Danny said 'Who are you to say what my right mind is?') When I called Danny's phone the message still said, *You have reached,* and then the robot voice stopped, *Danny,* he said, and then it resumed, *please leave a message at—*

If I meditated on Danny before I fell asleep, Millie said, he would come to me in dreams, bringing answers. If I put something of his beneath my pillow. If I only had the faith.

'You should go with them tonight,' Creed said. His paring knife halved a blood orange. 'Take a sweater. It's cold out.'

By the back door, they were already waiting. August was drawing a lunar calendar along the underside of her arm. Millie handed me my own jar. 'Come on,' she said, holding the door open.

First, Millie told me, they walked down the dirt road, all the way to the highway. If I got tired, she said, they would stop, and I said, 'No. I'll be fine.' The three of us headed down the gravel driveway, the half moon a sharp bite mark on the cheek of the sky. In the ditches along the roadside, the milk thistles had gone to seed. As we walked, now and then between the trees you could see the other houses, all the lights on in the windows, reckless and burning.

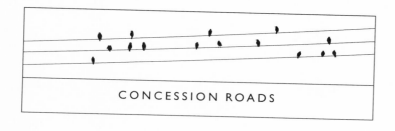

CONCESSION ROADS

If you listened to her long enough, you came to know who she was: Our Lady of Hard Luck. It was probably true. If she were a patron saint, she'd be for lost causes, answering the prayers of other girls like her. I imagined her as one of the holy women in religious paintings. Long white dress, pale halo, eyes rolled heavenwards, begged and beloved. But there was a beer bottle dangling from her French-manicured fingers by the neck, and the minute she opened her mouth, that vision shattered completely.

Her name was Sami and she always smelled like Amor Amor and cigarettes. She was staying down the road from my boyfriend, True, in Cedar Creek Mobile Home Estates, a trailer park on the edge of Lake Erie. True was always working—bartending at a place called Crash Landings, aviation-themed, with model airplanes dangling from the ceiling. On the walls were dusty photographs of old-time planes, uncrashed. *Aviation*, True said, was a word with roots in Latin—*avis* for bird. He had a thing for the dead language. (Sami said he always had liked useless things.) The theme was pretty grim and it wasn't a great bar, but it was the only one in town so they did steady business. I thought it must be so depressing, sitting there, drinking in the wreckage.

Anyway, True was gone a lot and I didn't know anyone else, so I was grateful for Sami. I was tired of being lonely. I met her the first night I came to stay with True. He invited her over. Old friends, he said. She showed up in a little dress that looked like lingerie, silky-slick and deep green, like an algae bloom over her skin. Dark shells of lace cupped her cleavage, low enough to show her black bra. She had blonde hair, white as milkweed silk, and a tattoo of Mickey Mouse right above her heart. After introductions, there wasn't much to say. True offered us shots of whisky, lined up the glasses and free-poured without spilling. He had ink on his knuckles, *love* and *hate* in a nautical font, a tribute to Robert Mitchum's killer preacher in *Night of the Hunter*. I thought someone who tattooed themselves like that, smack on the hands where anyone could see, was bold in a brave, dazzling way. It had been the first thing I noticed about him after his face.

'What are we drinking to?' Sami wanted to know.

'*Ad multos annos,*' he said, and we took the shots.

She licked her lower lip. She had a tongue ring that glittered when she talked and a habit of clicking it against her teeth or tapping it against one of her fake nails. 'What does that mean?'

'To many years.'

She snorted. 'Of this? No thank you.'

True collected the shot glasses. 'That's your problem,' he said. 'No joy in life.'

He introduced me as Cecilia, and she abbreviated it to Cee. That was how she called me over that first morning, when I was dragging the trash out to the side of the dusty road. *Cee! Hey, Cee, hey girl. Get on over here,* and soon I found myself at her place every afternoon when he went to work.

I had met True in the late spring, when I was still working at a dental office. After four years of university, I had nowhere else to go. While my friends went on to grad schools in Toronto, Hamilton, Ottawa, I stayed in the city I'd always been in and went to work each day on the third floor of a medical building, in an office that smelled of bleach and teeth. I wore crumpled scrubs I didn't iron, drank black coffee, and stood in line each day to shell out for the over-salted soup sold next to the pharmacy. My days consisted of shelving and re-shelving the same medical files over and over again, a job where the only tenuous connection to my English Lit degree was the alphabetical order the filing system relied on. I sent bills to patients who had neglected their payments, affixed with red warning stamps and ominous overdue stickers. Sometimes these bills were addressed to the families of patients who had died with their bills unpaid. Sometimes all the dead owed amounted to seven or eight dollars. But it didn't matter. We would send out the letter anyway.

True came in one day in May with a broken tooth. I crouched between the shelves of medical files and read through his. A lateral incisor on his left side was so badly broken the nerve had become exposed. He needed a root canal and also a crown. The left side of his face was bruised a deep shade of purple I had never seen on skin before. His mouth was swollen and he had a black eye. On his right hand he seemed to be missing fingers, or parts of them. At five o'clock, when I got out of the elevator, I found him standing in the lobby. Hockey game, he told me when I asked about his tooth, smiling in a way that made his fat lip split, like I'd have to be a sucker to believe it.

I wasn't used to men like True at all. I dated depressive types who had to get weepily drunk on craft beer before they could ever make a move or tell you how they felt about anything. True had dirty-blond hair he wore uncut and uncombed, and blue eyes you'd sell your soul to have—or to see yourself in. A pierced and tattooed prince. A week after we met, he had my number in his cell under *My Cecilia,* and every time he picked me up to go out, he brought me a single long-stemmed rose, red and perfect, wrapped in cellophane and smelling like plastic. He'd whistle the Simon & Garfunkel song 'Cecilia', and he'd ask if I was going to break his heart. I was pretty charmed, and when he suggested I quit my job so that we could spend the summer together, I did. He had seemed like someone who always knew the way. So I went with him.

True lived in what he called a dead-end town, where there was nothing to do but gape at the roadkill. He had meant to go to school but never did. When he asked me what I did and I told him about my degree, he looked at me with a mix of admiration and resentment. 'You must think you're pretty smart, don't you?'

'Not really,' I said. 'It was just the only thing I was good at.'

He called Sami a dead-end girl, even though she had been a lot of places, had travelled farther than him and me put together. She had lived in Montreal for a while, had gone from there to Toronto, and then she wandered, in her words, back down here, to the southern periphery of Ontario. 'You can take the dead-end girl out of the dead-end town …' he said. He left it unfinished.

In Montreal, Sami said, she had learned some French.

'Sure,' True said. '*Voulez-vous coucher avec moi?*'

Sami had only shrugged. 'More than you,' she'd said. 'Anyway, I would never say that. I would say, *J'ai envie de toi.*'

Sami loved Montreal, where she had gone to jazz festivals. She walked to Mont-Royal on weekends and bought feather earrings, vinyl records, all kinds of beautiful shoes—boots sequinned with glittering stars, red stilettos with a six-inch gold heel sharp and thin as a finishing nail, black heels that laced up to her thighs. She had lived by Saint Joseph's Oratory, a shrine with ninety-nine stone steps. The true believers climbed up on their knees. She used to love the votive chapel. She missed Montreal, referred to her time there as the last year of her life before her children came. Sometimes she just called it the last year of her life.

Now she lived in one of the park's three cottages. The other two were empty except, now and then, for the odd birdwatcher looking for a low-budget place to stay down the road from Point Pelee. Sami was renting her cottage cheap from an ex-boyfriend, Silvio, who, she said, was still in love with her but who was married recently to someone else. Sami told Silvio it was hopeless—she was not a girl who'd settle for the sidelines. But she did take the cottage.

Her cottage, like the other two, germinated nothing but neglect. The lawn consisted of weeds sprouting through the gravel.

The house was a spider-speckled white with a roof of asphalt shingles, loose like teeth in a mouth just punched. Inside it was damp and smelled of mildew. The cottage had last been decorated in lurid seventies tones, shades of a sickly body—bilious green and stomach-acid yellow and rusted orange like dried blood. There was a bulletin board by the rotary phone on the wall, empty except for a 1982 calendar from a car dealership in Leamington, and a handwritten note on a scrap of paper: *Brenda and I went out to find real men, love Cheryl.*

'I hope they found them,' Sami said. She sighed, tapped the ash from her cigarette. I knew what she left unsaid, that there wasn't much of a chance they had.

Sami had twin boys, Braden and Jett, and a daughter named Amberlin. They were all under the age of six—sticky, suspicious children, mumbling through mouthfuls of missing teeth, who often wore swimsuits in lieu of clothing. She called Amberlin *baby girl* and *Amber baby* and *pretty princess* when she was affectionate, and, more frequently, *Amberlin Joy* when she was angry or annoyed. When she was happy with her sons, she called them her princes. The children never seemed to sleep; they chewed their food and spit it back into chipped coffee mugs they carried around with them. They taped ripped garbage bags to their clothes. They fell in love with every piece of trash they found in the ditch along the road. They collected stones and pinecones and fish flies, pinched by the wings and still twitching between their grimy fingers. When these insects died and the husks of their bodies were lost to the weeds or blew away, the children wept for hours.

One of Sami's favourite subjects to talk about, those long mornings we sat on her porch, was bad parents, among them her latest ex-boyfriend, the father of her children. The boys, she confessed with regret, had their father's blond curls, so she shaved their heads constantly, not wanting to be reminded of him. She told me Elvis Presley was her one true love, that she would forever compare every man in her life to him, specifically as he was in *Wild in the Country.*

'Amberlin looks like you,' I said one day. We were sitting on her porch, like usual.

Sami shook her head. She had a pink plastic heart-shaped mirror in one hand and a nail file in the other. She'd cracked a tooth on a bottle of beer last night and was tidily filing it smooth. 'No, she don't. She looks like her father, my poor sweetheart. But if she's lucky she'll outgrow it.'

Motherhood had taken Sami by violent surprise—a hostage situation, she said—and she had weathered it as she might have weathered a knife to the throat—with fear, unwillingly, against herself. But now, though she often longed to leave them, whenever she did, she found herself wishing to be back with them. I sometimes babysat for her, having nothing much else to do while True worked in the evenings. When she went out, rhinestone *S* around her neck, thin bracelets rattling on her wrists halfway to her elbows, white eyeliner and talons tipped in gold, she moved with a certain swagger, with the quick machine-gun tap of leopard-print stilettos. She was like a lipsticked gangster, always with something to say. But in the afternoon heat, when we tanned, when Sami's skin turned the rich colour of butter cake while her children shrieked through the trees and she hollered at them to stay off the beach, she was different then. Tired, sprawled in a lawn chair, knees popped apart loosely, in a sun-stripped bikini top and pink-tinted aviator shades. When she stood up you could see her scar, smiling on her stomach. Cigarette passed from lips to hand and then crushed out in a beer bottle. She still always had something to say.

'Why're you always hanging out over there, anyway,' True asked one evening. 'You're not like her. You could go places.' But I wasn't going much of anywhere at all. Just trips at noon to the corner store by the town line road with the twins and Amberlin. We bought cigarettes for Sami, and I let the kids pick out nickel-and-dime candy in little paper bags. When we left, their fingers were speckled with sugar, their unbrushed mouths warm with the coppery smell of old pennies.

'She's my friend,' I said. It sounded childish when I said it out loud. We were having dinner, gelatinous bowls of Kraft Dinner, gone cold when True had been late coming home.

True smacked his hand against the bottom of the empty ketchup bottle. A watery red discharge spattered his macaroni. I'd forgotten to get groceries. 'What do you do all day, anyway, besides babysit for Sami?'

'You told me to quit my job.'

'I thought you would find something better,' he said. 'Or at least keep this place up. I thought you had your shit together when I met you.'

On Friday nights, when True wasn't working, Sami came over, because she and the kids liked to watch *SmackDown*. They knew the wrestlers' complicated histories, their tremendous rivalries, their bitter lists of loves and losses. The wrestlers bled, flexed, climbed into the ring to holler out Shakespearean soliloquies of betrayal, heartache, and revenge, then hit each other with plastic folding chairs.

'One of my high school teachers came into work today,' True said. The teacher had recognized him as True cut fruit into garnishes—wedges, slices, and half-moons, and lemon peels into yellow twists. *You were so well spoken*, the teacher had said, *so very articulate.*

'That's nice,' Sami said. Amberlin and Jett were busy spitting at each other, but Braden had fallen asleep on her lap.

'Is it? Like it was some kind of surprise to him.' He turned towards where I sat. 'Why the fuck shouldn't I be well spoken?'

As it was more and more often with True, I had no answer, or none that would appease him. In disgust he got up, disappeared into the kitchen.

'If you're planning on staying with him you'll just need to learn how to tell him to shut up, or ignore him.' Sami stroked Braden's buzzed hair, gazing at the television, where a pink-haired wrestler threw herself off the ropes, double-leg-dropped another woman. 'There's nothing else you can say when he gets like that. He wasn't brought up right.'

Towards the end of August, Sami found a new boyfriend, Jasey Cadeau. *Ride it out, cowboy*, he liked to say, *ride it out*. It was an adage meant for all occasions, from Braden getting bee stung to Sami arguing with her ex to me expressing dismay about a job market that didn't require knowledge of Medieval erotic literature, nor did it want to pay someone to write a dissertation on Plato's tripartite theory of the soul. After awhile, I realized I didn't even really want to, anymore. Write about those things. Think about them. It bothered me at first. Then less and less and less.

Jasey was fresh out of jail and always telling Sami and whoever else would listen how lucky he was to have her, the solidest woman he knew. 'I'm so happy she introduced herself to me,' he said, shaking his head back and forth, back and forth, as if disagreeing with someone unseen. 'No more trouble for me, man. No more trouble, period.'

True was unimpressed. 'If I were you I wouldn't fuck with him, Sami. Don't know why you bother. He's a loser, baby. Thinks he's some kind of real criminal. What do you see in him, anyway?'

Sami shrugged, but I knew what she saw. Jasey was someone who loved her more than she loved him.

Now that Jasey was around, I didn't see Sami as much. Saturday nights, though, the Def Leppard cover band Jasey drummed for had practice, and Sami invited us over.

Sami missed Montreal most in the summer, she said, and when we came over, she promised she'd make lattes, despite the August heat, like she used to order when she lived there, in the cafés of Little Italy.

True and I arrived at nine. Sami was on the phone, but she waved us towards some chairs in the kitchen. We sat down and I saw True's gaze flicking over the dishes crisp with old ketchup, the countertop littered with a discarded bra, junk mail, all the fake eyelashes Sami had peeled off.

'Silvio,' she said, rolling her eyes, after she'd hung up. 'Just checking in, he says. Again. He's got rental places all over Essex County. You think that would keep him busy.'

'So why did you decide to come to this one?' I asked.

Sami shrugged, smiled. At the kitchen counter, she poured steamed milk into three cups of espresso. 'Why not?'

In the living room, Amberlin and the twins had stripped the sofa of cushions. They jumped from pillow to pillow, shining a flashlight in each other's eyes and screaming. Their noses dripped constantly, but Sami didn't offer tissues or assistance. Independence was crucial, she asserted, and she lacked the time to coddle three young children. Occasionally, she would order them to wash their hands, but usually they didn't, and the thin pink slices of bologna they ate would be smudged darkly.

'Shouldn't they be in bed?' True asked. *Feral*, he called them, but only when we were alone. *She needs to try and do something with them.*

'It's summer,' I said. 'Don't all kids stay up late in the summer?'

'They need a routine,' True said.

'Oh, they have one.' In a tight floral sundress that tied in the front and bright red lipstick, Sami looked beautiful, like the dangerous girls on the covers of old detective pulp fiction.

'I can see that.'

'They want to stay up till Jasey gets home. They love him. He's so good with them, too.'

I looked at True's face, the breezy contempt, the tension in his jaw—a carnivore jaw, *carnivore*, Latin for 'flesh' and for 'devour'—and I saw then that they had been together before, True and Sami, maybe always had been, in one way or another, and that they would be together again. But by then, and to my slow surprise, it wasn't the loss of True that I felt like a kick to the jaw, but the loss of Sami.

I told myself I used to be luminous with knowledge, but now my skull was filled with shadows. It surprised me, how quickly it all went to dust. September showed up, and before I knew it, I'd let the due date pass by for the online classes I'd meant to enrol in, missed a chance to apply for a job in college administration that I didn't want anyway. It was just so easy to let things slip away, to lie back and let one day dissolve into the next. Summer was almost over. For the last few weeks in September, I sometimes still went over, usually when Jasey was out, and Sami and I smoked on the front steps together, watched reruns of wedding dress shows and cake-baking competitions and extreme home renovations. So when I came by one Friday and found her on the gravel driveway throwing her hot-pink zebra-print luggage into the trunk of Jasey's late-nineties Honda Civic, hollering across the lawn at the twins, Amberlin on her hip, I was surprised.

'Where are you going?' I asked, because we never went any-where, at least anywhere beyond the corner store selling *hunting fishing licenses worms and propane*, or the bar just down the dusty grey road. We never went anywhere requiring directions, bags packed, or any real plan beyond the present.

Sami fished a lighter out of her teal push-up bra, lit a cigarette. She was wearing the same dress she had been the night I had met her—the one that made her look like a mermaid with a gloss of green scales and seaweed over her skin. She was tanned the deep sweet shade of pumpkin pie now. She had cropped her bleach-blonde hair into something sharp and shoulder-length. She had lost some of the look she'd had when we met, the summery and lan-guid air, like wisteria wilting in the heat.

'We're getting out of here,' she said. 'Up to London for awhile.

Jasey has family there. He says he can get a job. He knows roofing.'

'Sure,' I said. I tried not to think about the fact that Jasey, with his flashy diamond earrings and ungrammatical tattoos and Merle Haggard *Mama Tried* t-shirt, might actually be more employable than I was.

Sami had a friend in London, too—Ava, who made and sold her own soaps at the Covent Garden Market. Sami was going to go work with her. 'I have all these ideas for soaps,' she said. 'A whole Canadian theme, you know? A bar that smells like maple syrup. An evergreen one. Something white, with glitter, maybe, like the new snow in December. A beachy soap that smells like Lake Erie.'

'You hate the lake.' She shrugged. 'I'll miss you, Sami,' I said.

She dragged the twins into the backseat by the elbows, strapped Amberlin into a car seat, stood up. 'Text me, Cee. You can come and visit.' But even as she said it, smiled, we both knew I'd never go. Sorry for myself and half in love with Sami, I watched her take her place beside Jasey and wave goodbye, her hand a gleam of silver out the car window.

Holding on is hard. You get tired, you give out. It is just so easy to let things slip away, to fade into a haze of endless sunsets. It's a slow slide into stasis, sessility.

'From Latin, *stessilis*, which means sitting, which is all you ever do,' True said. I was paralyzed, like an insect lured by sweet water to the lips of pitcher plants, dreamy and drowned.

'She'll be back,' True said that night as we sat in front of the television. And maybe he was right or maybe he wasn't, but in the end it didn't matter. All that mattered was that she'd gone.

FIRST, DO NO HARM

At first I thought I was still asleep, the choking a dream. I knew that sound. A finger caught in a throat like a needle jumping on a vinyl record. The stuck, dragging sound. I'd been that body all my life, damaged grooves that could never play the music right. Why some brains seem to hum nothing but 'Here Comes the Sun' on a smooth loop while others only get some atonal drone, barely back-masked messages of self-annihilation, I never understood. The retching kept going as my dreams receded, and I stumbled from my bed. By the time I got there, to the bathroom down the hall, my daughter stood at the sink, brushing her teeth, lips flecked with mint-green paste.

'I think I caught something.'

'Oh,' I said. Sunlight seeped through the faux-wood blinds; they were supposed to be moisture-resistant, but you could see they were already warping. 'Are you all right? Are you staying home today?' The light struck the bathroom mirror, smudged because Ophelia still liked to write in the shower steam; the bevelled edges, acting like prisms, left a small rainbow on her hair, another one wavering along the back of her hand.

'No, I'm going to class. I feel much better now.' Tilting her head to the side, Ophelia began plaiting her long dark hair into a fishtail braid. Her fingers faltered.

'Are you sure? I can call in at work and stay home with you, if you need me.'

'Aureline's on her way to pick me up. We have a class at nine.' She looked at me, a bobby pin between her teeth. 'Don't get excited. I wasn't feeling great, that's all. I'm not making a habit of this.'

I didn't say anything. It was a little true and a little untrue, the way the meanest things are. Because my first thought had been almost like relief. Years of cognitive behaviour therapy had not undone the knots I'd tied, expunged the feelings of release I felt for myself or anyone else as they heaved. *You're free.* It hadn't erased the feeling that sickness had subtracted some of the damage done throughout the day, had tidied up the sums a bit, like a swift accountant could. Balancing the body's books.

Horrible, reflexive or not. Because of course I didn't want that for my daughter. The calloused knuckles, the dull teeth I bleached and bleached, the fainting and the ulcers, when things were at their worst. All the loathing and remorse and the love, too, all the wasted, abashed love. It all goes down the drain. Even before she was born I'd been scared that I could pass on to her my own bad habits. I prayed, made promises to watch myself. One person's clouds can rain on generations.

———————

I'd been thinking of skipping the meeting that night, for group therapy. I hated to go. I was in it, mostly, for Ophelia, who'd begged me, crying, just over a year ago. *Get some help.* I'd been sitting on the edge of the bathtub, dizzy, still wiping spit from my lips. How could I say no? Of course I'd go; I'd do anything to comfort her, because what kind of mother did this to her daughter? I knew then that although I thought I'd been so secretive, so neat, she must have heard me throwing up for years. I hated to go, but the thoughts that had come to me this morning, as if they were natural, sickened me.

I drove to therapy after work, parked my car at the far end of the lot. Although I'd come here for a year, I was still the same—it was embedded in me to take these little extra steps, maximizing calories burnt, one of those tips extolled as good sense in countless magazines. Like always take the stairs, drink water, step on a scale every day. Helpful little hints.

The meetings took place on the third floor, over the city market. I took the stairs, reciting the mental list of everything I'd eaten that day, as I did every day, assigning a quick grade (*good* and *bad* were harsh, judgmental words they told us, in therapy, not to ever use). In the room where we met, the chairs were arranged in a circle, most already filled with bodies. A photocopied package lay on the one empty chair, waiting. Self-consciously I picked up the papers and sat down, shoulders hunched. The top paper had *Recovery* printed in black script across the front. I drew a pen from my purse; we were encouraged to take notes. I sketched a smiling face as if willing myself towards happiness.

A finger reached down, tapped the happy face. 'Positive affirmation. That's great.' I looked up to see a man standing there, wearing a collared shirt the clean green of sliced cucumbers, a tailored cardigan. Thick-framed tortoiseshell glasses like you'd see on a father from the 1950s, but he was young. 'I'd like to welcome everyone tonight. You've all taken an incredible step already by being here. My name's Palmer Aspen, and I'm honoured to be temporarily attempting to begin where Dawn left off. She's gone on an early maternity leave.'

A murmur of welcome from some of the girls. Palmer took a seat. 'Dawn left stellar notes, but I'll be looking to you for some guidance, of course. I believe you start each session with what she called a check-in.'

We did, a dreaded time where Dawn interrogated us about our emotions. 'Are you aware of how you are feeling?' she wanted to know. I felt like a cross-examined witness caught lying. But we couldn't say that. Dawn thought that was the problem, or part of it. That we weren't conscious of our feelings, informed of our emotions. But I knew the opposite was true. We were here because we felt too much, and we knew we did. We'd tried all kinds of ways to stop feeling.

'And you could add a little introduction—just your name if

you'd like. But I'm interested in getting to know all of you. Why don't we start here, to my left?'

'I'm indifferent,' Cally said. On the photocopied sheet we'd received at our first visit, we'd been given an emotion chart to choose from, each illustrated by a cartoon face. *Indifferent* was lowered lids, raised eyebrows, mouth slanted coolly. Which was more or less the expression Cally maintained at our meetings. 'And my name's Cally. I'm twenty. I'm only here because my boyfriend threatened to break up with me if I don't get some help. He thinks I'm too skinny.' She said this last bit with a trace of pride. 'But really, who cares. I just don't, anymore.'

Palmer nodded, slowly. 'I'm hearing that in your voice.'

Cally nodded. 'It's just, I was doing so well,' she said, picking at her yellow nail polish. 'Like, with this whole thing, the purging, you know, and things with my boyfriend were in a good place, finally, and this weekend I was stupid—I got drunk, really drunk, and we had a big fight. I ended up going home and eating ice cream with my hands, and throwing it all up.'

The rest of us exchanged looks briefly. Cally had broken at least two key rules of the group, as laid out by Dawn. Last week she had explained MDMA to us. 'It's like Ecstasy,' she said, before Dawn cut her off. 'We don't talk about substance abuse here.'

We also weren't supposed to get explicit about what we did when we weren't here. You talked about it vaguely, in euphemistic terms. A circle of us, veiled as brides. 'Well, I didn't exactly meet all the goals I set.' 'There was a relapse.' Or, 'I think I need to journal more, my emotions....' You could never say what Cally said. What we all wanted to say. 'I puked my fucking guts up. Sometimes I want to die.' I glanced over at Palmer, nodding calmly, taking it all in, one finger resting against the curve of his lower lip.

'Cally's not supposed to bring up her drug addiction here,' Ashley complained, sticking up her hand like we were in class.

'I don't have an addiction.'

Palmer held up his hands. 'We all have our tactics, which we use to subvert reality at times,' he said. 'That's why we're here. Because all of us can understand that need. We are here to find better methods, healthier approaches, but I'm not here to censor you. That's counterproductive. Cally, thank you for your honesty.' He looked at me. 'Are you ready to go next?'

I pressed my stack of papers flat across my knees. I was still dressed from work: a tailored indigo skirt, dark stockings, a long grey cardigan, a strand of graduated pearls. I felt suddenly how brittle and finicky I must have looked next to these long-legged girls, nineteen, twenty, in the right jeans and leggings, birds tattooed on their wrists, scarves slouched perfectly around shoulders. 'Um, yes. All right. I'm all right, I guess. That's all—that's all I can say, really.'

Dawn never liked my choices. '"All right" isn't an emotion,' she said. 'It's meaningless. Try something else.'

'All right,' I said, 'I mean—I'm okay.'

'Not an emotion.'

'I'm good.'

'A judgment word. We don't use those here.'

'I'm miserable,' I said.

Dawn nodded. 'Miserable' was all right. It was on the pre-approved list of feelings, complete with a round face, its mouth a crumpled squiggle. As soon as I spoke, I knew I'd screwed up; I waited for Palmer, like Dawn, to correct me. But instead he only smiled kindly. 'Sometimes that sums it up, doesn't it.' I nodded, carefully. 'And what about your name?'

'Kathleen.'

'Kathleen, thank you,' he said. One more smile. 'It's good to meet you. And next we have ...'

'Kendall,' she said. 'I'm confident today, I think....'

———

For a month of Thursday nights, I went to group willingly. Not trying to be a good mother, which was the only reason I had gone before. I was beyond hope of helping myself. I'd stopped believing in a cure long ago.

I went because I was incurable, in more ways than one. I went to hear Palmer say 'Kathleen, welcome,' while reaching to take the evening's photocopies and knowing that his hand would for a moment touch my own and that, as I held my papers and home-work on my lap, ready to take notes, the fingers on that hand would burn an hour afterward. I went each week to learn about him. He was newly graduated from university, with a master's degree in Social Work from the University of Windsor. He taught restorative yoga on the weekends, he loved mid-century modern design. He had recently acquired a set of tulip chairs with mustard-yellow cushions, real Eero Saarinen originals. 'Can you believe it?' he asked us. Sometimes, he said, he just couldn't believe his luck.

The fifth Thursday, I was the first one to leave after group. We weren't encouraged to socialize with each other, but I didn't want to take any chances, stumble into some accidental small talk while siz-ing each other up in the elevator, tallying bones. I took the stairs, but in the lobby I went left, through the doors of the market.

A display of seedless watermelons, of overripe, bruised peaches. The butcher's counter, the red glisten of raw meat under glass, the wet shine of naked hearts on metal trays. At the florist I stopped, thinking of Ophelia, how this had once been her favourite part of the market. In group we were encouraged to nurture and reward ourselves. We'd been given a list of suggestions. We could wear perfume, or paint our nails. We could take a bath or buy our-selves some flowers. I looked around and saw nothing but flowers slowly wilting in buckets of stale water, limp stalks of hyacinths, tulips drooping.

'Kathleen?' I looked up. Palmer was standing there, hands in the pockets of his cardigan. 'How are you?'

'Is this a check-in?'

He laughed a little. 'No, no, I was just wondering, you know. I'm glad we crossed paths. I like your energy.'

From someone else it would have seemed cheesy, cheap, a relic pick-up line. 'Thank you,' I said, because he seemed so sincere. Because I liked his energy, too.

He cleared his throat. 'Well, how are you doing? With, you know, your goals.'

That morning, I'd waited for what seemed like hours for Aureline to pick Ophelia up, and rushed to the bathroom once she had. After, I'd felt good for an hour, high and untouchable. 'I'm meeting my goals.'

'Really? That's wonderful.'

'For the most part.'

'But I bet it's not easy.'

The tulips, nestled in cellophane, smelled waxy and sweet, tucked next to long stalks of gladiolas, foxglove. Behind the glass counter the florist was wrapping the green stems of roses for a wedding, removing all the thorns.

'No,' I said. 'Some days are harder than others.'

'You know, it helps if you stay busy. Keep your mind off of.... There's a show at the Detroit Institute of Arts. The Dutch Masters. Maybe you'd want to go?'

'The still lifes of breakfasts, right?' I asked. 'Those monochromatic bowls of fruit.'

'You're right, there'll be a lot of still life paintings, I think. Cutlery, flowers, candles. Allegorical depictions of the brevity of our existence.'

'So monochromatic bowls of rotting fruit.'

'There's more, too, I think. Landscapes of ruins. Herdsmen tending cattle.'

I was still holding my papers. There were more suggestions listed to nurture ourselves this week. Buy new makeup. Window shop. Small, bloodless joys. I looked at Palmer, thought about my alternatives for the evening. Lemon water, the endless treadmill, reruns from the nineties. Fat Monica on *Friends*, her body the punch line. Deferring the yearning to purge, over and over again.

'Yes,' I said. 'I'll go with you.'

———————————

When I came downstairs the next night, just before Palmer had said he'd come by, I found Ophelia and Tamás lying on opposite ends of the living room sofa. The radio was on, but it wasn't playing music. Instead it was buzzing loudly.

Ophelia quickly sat up. 'I didn't know you were here.'

'Is there something wrong with the radio?'

Now Tamás sat up, too, but slowly, the way he tended to move. He wore his glasses always on a slight diagonal, apparently unaware they were crooked. He had the thin, pale look of a plant that had grown without enough sunlight. 'We're listening to Cosmic Microwave Background Radiation.'

Ophelia drew her knees up close to her chest. Her eyelids were brushed with some kind of gold shadow. 'Objects in space sending out electromagnetic waves.'

'And you find this … interesting?'

'Thought provoking,' Tamás said. 'It opens up our minds.'

'Sometimes you can hear a meteorite fall,' Ophelia said.

'Really.' Tamás looked overdue for a haircut again; he always looked a little shabby around the edges. I tried to pretend I didn't see the gold dust on his cheeks. He was Ophelia's friend from childhood, who lived just down the street. My amity towards him had waned over the years. He was aimless, shifting from one job to another, saying he would go to school next semester but never seeming to go. Last winter he had walked into the kitchen as I was trying to fill in my weekly goal-setting worksheet before group. The key was to take small steps, the paper said, assuring us even the largest of goals could be accomplished this way. I closed my note-book, but not before he'd had a look.

'You know, on Mars you'd weigh less than half of what you do here,' he'd said. 'Better avoid Jupiter, though; you'd weigh the most there.' He stood there like he belonged in my kitchen, Ophelia lingering behind him

'Don't you have school today?' I'd asked. They were dressed in their uniforms, white shirts untucked over dress pants, a grey wool kilt. I'd resisted the urge to straighten Ophelia's pin, her navy blue knee socks. Anyway, she was out of my reach.

He'd shrugged. 'We just wrote our English exam.' Tamás had ink stains on his shirt, his hands. Hair in his eyes. I wondered how his mother could stand it. When they were young, we'd been friends. Lili had always been immaculate, wearing slim yellow-gold chain necklaces over silk dresses. She always looked perfect, each detail bespoke, even doing her yard work. She wore rubies and sapphires. The hardest precious stones, she had told me once.

'Don't you have another one tomorrow to study for, then?'

'Ancient history,' he'd said. 'I already know everything.'

'That must be nice.'

Tamás had smiled. 'It is,' he'd said. 'But it can be quite the encumbrance as well. Especially when you're seventeen.'

Now, Ophelia looked at me. 'Where are you going, anyway? You look nice.'

'Out, with a friend.'

'A date,' she said. 'Do I know him?'

I fixed my gaze in the foyer mirror. After deliberating for an overly long time, I'd chosen a long dress in a watercolour floral print, gold heels, a thin gold necklace hanging just below my collar-bone. I concentrated on my lipstick. Pink. It was supposed to be a safe shade. Ophelia went around wearing whatever; she didn't seem to care. Lately she favoured purple. 'No,' I said, slipping the lipstick into my purse. 'His name is Palmer. I just met him.'

My daughter narrowed her eyes. 'Where?'

I couldn't say work, the bridal salon. She'd know it was a lie. 'A few months ago,' I said carefully.

'You never go anywhere. Except your meetings. It wasn't there, was it? What is he, a bulimic?'

'Actually, he's more like someone who helps lead our group.'

'So he's the therapist? I thought you weren't even supposed to socialize.'

'With each other,' I said. 'The other patients.' This was another core rule of Dawn's: contact outside the group was firmly discouraged. It hadn't been an issue before; I doubted Cally was trying to friend me on Facebook—me, awkward, pushing forty, in a prissy cardigan, who thought M D M A was a form of mixed martial arts.

'Aren't they supposed to take some kind of oath? *First, do no harm.*'

'That's doctors, I think. And anyway, he isn't doing any *harm.*'

And she said, 'How can you even say that?' Glancing towards Tamás, as if for some support, but he was lying back down, his eyes already closed.

———————

The Dutch Masters had their own wing at the art gallery. Many were there for the season only, on loan. White wall after white wall of gold-framed Vanitas paintings. Skulls painted amidst bowls and silverware and tulips, girls with fragile butterfly wings. Life was short, these painters knew; the things you thought of as luxuries or pleasures were cold and hollow. Motifs of rotten fruit and bird skeletons, hourglasses and smoke. *Still Life*, oil on wood, by Willem Claesz Heda, 1634, a lemon already half unpeeled. *An Allegory of the Vanities of Human Life*, oil on oak panel, by Harmen Steenwyck. *Still Life with Turkey Pie*, oil on panel, 1627, by Pieter Claesz. Poppies and plum leaves, marigolds in blue bowls. *Vanity of vanities, all is vanity.*

What I always remember about the tunnel is the lights. Now, and when I was a child, when my father would say, 'Here we are. Now we're in the States,' at the very point we crossed over. They marked the place on the tiles, the Canadian flag, the American. We used to go over to Detroit to visit his aunt. 'And here we are, home again.' The bright lights of Goyeau as you exited the tunnel, dim, always, after Detroit and the cool glitter of its skyscrapers, the Renaissance Center, the Art Deco Penobscot…

On the way back, Palmer and I got stuck in traffic in the tunnel. In the middle, where the radio dissolved into static, a cacophony of noise. I wondered if it was strange to love words so much. I remembered the exact moment I learned the definition of *cacophony* (sitting in my grade two classroom, reading about the dissonance of birds in an aviary). I used to study the dictionary, obsess over adjectives. Now I couldn't remember the last time I'd read a book.

We talked as we drove down Wyandotte, about the paintings we'd seen, others we liked; '*The Scream*,' I said. As for him, he liked the Pre-Raphaelite paintings.

'*The Awakening Conscience*,' I said. '*Found*.'

'No, not those ones. More like, Millais's *Ophelia*, or *The Lady of Shalott*.'

I knew those girls. Dreamy and drowned. Inert, transfixed on the middle distance, pale hands limply touching elegant throats, their long hair.

'Can I see you again? There's this class at a studio in Walkerville next Friday on book binding—'

'I'd like to see you again.'

'It's not that late yet. Maybe you'd like to get coffee.…'

In group they made us ask ourselves questions every week. *Are you making healthy choices?* 'I'd love to see those chairs you were telling me about. The tulip chairs. I think my great aunt had a set in her kitchen.'

'Well, they're not in perfect condition,' he said apologetically. 'They've yellowed a bit at the bases. One chair has some light gouging....'

I said it was all right, it would be fine, I could imagine them flawless. 'We all have some light gouging, anyway.' He laughed. In group, Dawn coached us about self-care, the things we did to restore ourselves. We learned how important it was to avoid your triggers, to be able to cope. Palmer parked the car in a shaded driveway. Journaling, watching the sunrise, baking, window shopping, what they called 'me time', which seemed to consist of bubble baths and manicures.

I followed Palmer up the sidewalk, the porch steps. Inside, as we crossed the threshold, as the door closed, Palmer seemed troubled. His hands fumbled as he took off his coat.

'Here, let me help you,' I said, loosening a button. Maybe too motherly. He wore a camel hair coat, a scarf checked with cream and burgundy. In my six-inch heels I was taller than him. His lips met my collarbone and that was where he put his mouth first. My left clavicle. The most broken bone in the human body.

'Kathleen,' he said, 'if anything we did put your recovery at risk, I couldn't forgive myself.'

And I said, 'It won't.' I didn't say what I really thought: that I would never recover, either way.

'Maybe I could even help you, you know....'

'Of course. I'm sure you could.'

He brightened. 'I had a paper published, about the importance of social supports in patients with—I mean not that ... I don't mean to offend—I don't see you like that, a patient. Sick. I mean I would never....'

I nodded, to say *I know, of course*. I thought about joking, *Because if you did see me as a patient ...* But I knew not to. That it would rattle him completely. A little deceit was necessary, considerate, even, most days. To ourselves and to others. You don't have to think of it as deception, only a benevolent sort of pretence. So I said, 'All we have is the moment we're in. We're not alive in the past, or the future.' That was something I had learned in group. Dawn liked to tell us that. Mindfulness, she called it. If only we could stop ruminating morosely over the past, or cowering before the future. If we could forgive ourselves for our disgraces, then we could learn to be happy. Maybe we could finally be at peace. *Breathe,* she always reminded us, as if that were all we needed. To keep breathing. 'Close your eyes,' I said. 'Think of what you want now. In the moment.' Palmer nodded. I closed my eyes too. 'Breathe,' I added. He did, he breathed in, and so did I. I loved the way he smelled: bitter orange and juniper.

When I opened my eyes again, his were still closed. I watched the pale curve of his eyelashes, the soft lift of his chest under his open coat as he breathed. Thought about the way some of us moved, like fire, making quick and unkind work of everything we touched. And then I thought about the way others, certain of their rightness, of the goodness in their hearts, all the ones that thought they were so pure—did their own damage, never knowing, never wanting to. Meaning no harm, they caused it all the same.

It's not the ending that addicts crave. Not the sickness, the regret, the clumsy shame. It's only the beginning that is so beguiling. The first sweet spark, shining in the dark. The initial moment of relief, yes, and of hope. That this time, it will be different. This time, I will find a way to fix it all …

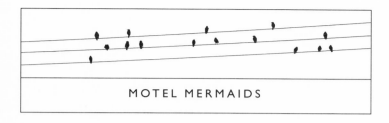

MOTEL MERMAIDS

Liss said, 'We are motel mermaids; we are made of magic.' Which sounded better than the reality that we were housekeeping for the Blue Haven Motel on an island in the middle of Lake Erie. During the day Liss showed me how to play hearts and we did what she called 'keeping up appearances', which meant we went to work on any obvious dirt and left the rest. The worst was when we found bloodstains, because then you had to change the sheets, or maybe it was the sand, because that got everywhere. Liss said if you didn't want any sand, you wouldn't come to the beach, so it was okay if we didn't get all of it. It was part of the experience. In the same way, it was all right if we couldn't get the lake smell out of the rooms or the dampness from the bedding. People came here because they loved nature, Liss said, not because they were looking for a five-star experience. But we still got some complaints. It bothered me, but it didn't bother Liss. It bothered Sal, though, and he let us know, tensely, whenever complaints arose. He didn't call them complaints, though, he called them *concerns*. Liss would laugh, and tell him to relax; she could get away with that, because he was her boyfriend.

'We're dating brothers, so that makes us like sisters,' Liss said. I wanted to believe it. She was sitting on the unmade bed, flipping through a magazine that she had found, *Ladies' Home Journal*. People left a lot of things behind in motel rooms. The deck of cards was laid out between us, another treasure Liss had found in a bedside drawer. They were slightly wavy from water damage and had pictures of the island's ferry on the backs. She was reading excerpts from *Can This Marriage Be Saved?* '"I feel so terrible for what Janie's going through, but I don't actually like, want to stop fucking around on her or anything."'

'It doesn't say that.'

Liss winked at me. She had dark eyes accentuated by the fake lashes she glued on every day, and the extravagant facial expressions of a silent-movie star, her eyebrows acting as punctuation, like she'd just slunk off the silver screen in a gold sequinned gown. She wore off-the-shoulder tops and these mirrored aviator shades, and she always smelled like coconut milk. When she talked she put her hands all over you. You'd jump a bit, like a little shock, a spark. It was incredible. She drew you in, and you wanted to tell her everything, your whole life story, like she would understand. I always held back, but I knew why Sal loved her, and why Mickey loved her, too.

Sal was growing a moustache that summer, which Liss hated.

'It makes you look like a sleaze,' she said.

'Maybe I am a sleaze,' he said.

'You obviously are,' Liss said. 'But you don't have to advertise it.'

They were always going back and forth at it. That evening, before the moustache, it was because Liss had bought beer in bottles.

'I told you to get the cans,' Sal said. 'Someone always breaks a bottle, and then I've got to clean up the mess.'

Liss didn't look up from the sofa where she was painting her toenails with peach glitter polish. 'Well, then, you go next time.'

'I would have gone tonight, but someone has to do the dishes.'

Liss flicked the brush at the lip of the bottle. 'I'll wash them.'

'No, you don't wash the dishes right.'

'Clean is clean.' Liss shrugged her bare shoulders. Her toenails gleamed in the bleary light from the kitchen, a lone bulb burning out beneath a leaded-glass lampshade.

'The problem is you don't take any pride in your work.'

Liss didn't look up from the second coat she was slowly applying. 'It must be nice, knowing what everyone else's problems are.
Maybe you should take a look at your own some time.'

'I'm looking at the source of all my problems right now.'

Mickey couldn't handle it. He would shut himself up in our
bedroom while they argued all over the cottage. When I went in
that night he was lying in bed, watching an episode of *Wheel of Fortune*. On top of the dresser, we had a television the size of a toaster
that only seemed to ever show game shows, and Mickey was
addicted to them. He had a very addictive personality.

'I knew we shouldn't have come here,' he said as I closed the
door.

I wanted to ask, *Then why did we?* but I didn't. Money, I guess,
or to prove something to Sal—that Liss was powerless to affect
him. But I knew the truth. He was still stuck in symbiosis, but she
had moved on. Heinrich Anton de Bary defined symbiosis as 'the
living together of unlike organisms'. I remembered that from high
school biology, a little. Fungi and beetles. Sharks and remora. The
little red-billed birds perched on the backs of rhinoceroses, picking
them clean.

I sat down on the edge of the bed. It must have been an old
episode because Vanna had this frosted lavender eyeshadow and
her blonde hair was all feathery and she was tan in a very eighties
way, like she was on the cover of *Vanna Speaks*, which my mother
borrowed from the library when we were kids, to read by the
Riverside Centennial pool while we swam in the afternoons. Vanna
was looking extremely glamorous and smiling a lot as she revealed
the letters one by one. I lay down and thought maybe Mickey would
put an arm around me at least, but he was pretty into the show. The
category was 'Husband & Wife'. I could tell it was Lucille Ball and
Desi Arnaz, but I didn't say anything. When I was younger, my
mom told me they ended up divorced in real life, and I was still

kind of sad about it. I used to watch *I Love Lucy* and had always liked the way Lucy and Ricky bickered a bit and teased each other; they gave each other a hard time, but you could feel that, at the end of the day, they really loved each other, and that when Ricky called out, *Lucy, I'm home*, they were actually happy about it. Or that's what I had believed, before my mother told me. It was a letdown that stayed with me even now, at twenty; it was the first time I had ever doubted true love.

Everything on our television looked murky and blue, like the set of *Wheel of Fortune* was underwater. Vanna glided across the screen like a mermaid in her silver sequins. I could smell the warm cherry scorch of cough syrup on Mickey's breath. 'Do you want to do something?'

'Like what?'

'I don't know. Maybe we could go for a walk?'

'I'm pretty fucked up right now, Miri.'

'Yeah,' I said, sitting up again. 'That's cool. No problem. Well, maybe I'll just go outside for a bit, you know. Get some fresh air.'

'Have fun,' Mickey mumbled, or I thought that was what he said. It was hard to tell when he was numbed down to his tongue.

The rest of the cottage was dark. The windows were open and there was a breeze coming in from the lake. I liked how you could hear it at night, the low steady ebb and flow. It was like a lullaby, water on stone. Liss was gone. She had probably left for the bar with the American girls we'd met earlier while tidying up their motel room. Empty bottles glittered on the kitchen table. The dishes Sal had washed shone, drying in the rack.

When I stepped outside I was surprised to see Sal, sitting in one of the plastic chairs in the gravel by our front door. We were staying in a low, squarish white cottage on the edge of the motel property. He leaned back in his lawn chair, looking up at the stars.

'Looks like me and you got the same problem, Miri.' He was

still looking up at the sky. It reminded me of something Liss had said to me once. How she'd been walking to meet Sal and she had seen, for the first time, a shooting star, and she knew it was a sign. 'A sign of what?' I asked, and she grabbed my hand, held it to her chest. I remember feeling her heart beating there, the force of her blood hard against my palm. She'd been wearing a set of thin gold stacking rings on her trigger finger and they cut into my knuckle with the pressure. 'That we were meant to be,' she said, her hand still on mine. 'That we were not a mistake.'

By the water, it was cooler at night. The lake was sighing over the stony beach across the dirt road. The sky looked like a kindergarten art project—blue indigo paint, silver glitter everywhere. Behind us in the field, the long grass crackled with insects. Down the road you could hear the music from the bar, too. Liss was probably there, dancing.

'What is that?' I asked Sal. 'Our problem.'

'We fall in love too easy,' he said.

———————

Love is a stimulant at first, a sedative later. But I only think like that now. Before Mickey, I was constantly in love. Despite knowing how Ricky and Lucy had ended up, I still believed, or wanted to believe in a love like salvation, an everlasting love.

I met Mickey on the city bus, coming home from my classes at the university, eastbound on the 1C. At first I didn't really notice him. I had my backpack on my lap and was reading *Paradise* by Toni Morrison and trying to take notes with a pen that was bleeding ink all over my paper, all over my hands, when I heard his voice.

'Excuse me?'

Across the aisle, I saw Mickey for the first time. He was sitting with his legs apart, hunched over with his elbows on his knees, his jeans frayed at the knees and the hems. A pair of red Converse high-tops on his feet and a black knit hat pulled low over dark curls.

'I'm trying to get to Pillette,' he said. 'When do I get off?'

I glanced out the window. 'That was awhile back, I'm sorry—we're almost in Forest Glade.'

'I think I'm lost,' he said, sliding one hand half under his hat, rubbing his disorderly curls. 'If I get off now, can I walk there?'

'It'll take a bit.'

'That's all right.' He had this tilting smile, crooked teeth and a fat lower lip. 'I don't have nothing else to do.'

We got off at the next stop together, by Tecumseh Mall. Mickey asked for directions. He was staying with his cousins for now, he said, and he wasn't used to the city. He'd lived all his life by the lake.

Then he said, 'Hey, well—if you have a little time, maybe I can buy you a coffee or something. Like a thank-you. For helping me.'

'You don't have to thank me.'

'Then maybe you just wanna have a drink with me,' he said. 'Now, or sometime later ...'

'Now is good,' I said. That smile hit me in the stomach, a sucker punch.

May was the month of emeralds, of lily of the valley, the twin month. It was also the month of Mary, Liss told me when I met her. *Mother most pure, pray for us.* Liss went to mass each Sunday at Our Lady, Star of the Sea. She said I could come with her to mass if I wanted, in the little white church on the south side of the island.

Liss was waiting for us when we got off the ferry Monday evening, in the middle of a wreck of gulls. She was wearing an olive-green dress tied around the waist and around the wrists in two tight bows, a pair of gold-strapped wedge heels and her aviator shades pushed back atop her dark hair. She came to me and Mickey first, crushing our hands. 'I'm so glad you're here,' she said, looking at us. Mickey said nothing, but loosened his hand from hers with a snap of his wrist, giving it a reflexive rub against his jeans, like someone trying to dull the sting of an insect bite.

Back on the ferry, Mickey had slumped at a cafeteria table, drinking pop mixed with whisky till he fell asleep. 'Come with me,' Sal said. 'Let's go up on deck.' So we did. I stood beside him, watching the grey-green waves. He was wearing grey linen shorts and a white crewneck shirt and these expensive-looking sunglasses. I'd never known any guy our age to dress as nicely as Sal did. I wondered if he was actually a lot older than us. When I thought he wasn't looking, I tried to study his face, but I could never tell. 'It's a good thing Mickey decided to come,' Sal said, one hand on the railing, squinting in the sunlight. 'He needs something to do.'

I liked the way Sal talked, so confidently. Like maybe he would know how to help Mickey, because I was at a loss.

Now we were here, and here was Liss. Something about her reminded me of the promise of summer in late spring, that hopefulness. *Any day now.* A coppery shimmer to her already, like she'd spent days at the beach. *O rose of May! Dear maid, kind sister.* The gulls screamed and circled around us, a flock of mouthy angels. She was still holding my hand.

'Come on,' she said. 'You can come with me, Miri. I'll show you around. Sal and Mickey have a lot of catching up to do.' So I followed her across the dirt road, leaving them behind. When I glanced back, I could see Sal was talking to Mickey, a hand on his shoulder; but Mickey was looking back towards the lake, in the direction we'd come from, as if searching for the unseen shore.

Liss opened the cottage door, flicked on the lights. There was one main room with a kitchen in one corner and a pair of slumping sofas in another. The floor was a waxy, once-gold linoleum. Then there was a tenebrous little hallway, where the washroom was, and also our bedrooms, directly across from each other.

'This is your room.' Liss held out her hand, palm up, led the way inside. It smelled like mildew and stale cigarettes. It contained a twin bed with sheets from the sixties, in a mod floral print, matching curtains in the window. There was a dresser with a mirror gone cloudy from years of lakeside humidity, and a single folding chair in the corner, leaning up against the wall.

Liss glanced around the room briefly. In the mirror she was only a dark nebulous shape. 'We can play cards, if you want. Do you know how to play hearts?'

'No.'

'I can teach you,' she said. 'I'll go get the cards.' The cottage was quiet and I wondered where Mickey and Sal were. Our bedroom window faced the dirt road, and then the lake. Liss came back, shuffling the cards. We would have to amend the deck, she said; we would have to take out the jacks and kings and certain numbers, because hearts was a game for three or even four people, but it would be all right. I sat down on the bed with Liss, and she divided the cards. Our coming here, she said, was the answer to her prayers. 'I've been so lonely.' Holding her cards to her chest, her dark eyes shining. 'Do you think some people are just prone to loneliness? Somehow more susceptible, like they lack the immunity for it?'

It surprised me a little. 'Isn't Sal staying here with you?'

'It's not the same.' Liss was used to living with her mother and sisters, she said, to being around her friends—and now here, on the island, at the motel, she felt herself drifting. The cruellest thing you could do to a girl, she said, was deprive her of the company of other women. 'But now you're here with me.' Smiling, one hand on mine. 'I can already tell that we're going to be good for each other, that we could really be friends. Just don't let it be weird between us.'

And I promised that it wouldn't be.

What bothered me sometimes was how Liss, usually after she was burning up from drinking whisky with Sal, would pull me aside into her little bedroom across the hall from ours. Their room almost identical to ours, down to the bedding—blowsy flowers, mustard yellow and earthy shades of brown, hazy light from a single bulb. Except their bed was made, every corner tucked in firm and neat, and ours was a heap of blankets and sheets, and there was no dirty laundry on their damp carpet.

With a brittle flicker of her dark lashes, mouth full of concern, she'd ask, 'How is Mickey?'

'He's fine,' I'd say, avoiding her gaze.

Liss and Sal had a dresser, too, the twin image of ours, minus the television set on top playing game shows on loop. There were four copper chevron handles on the drawers, mid-century modern style. Sal said the cottage was full of little touches like that, retro details that we could really appreciate if we only knew where to look.

Sometimes, relief would wash over her, like waves sluicing the sand smooth at the edge of the beach. Other days, I knew she didn't believe me. 'Are you helping him?'

When he asked for another beer, I went to get him one. When he said, 'Miri, get on my level,' I drank to catch up.

'I'm trying,' I'd say, and Liss would sigh.

'I know,' she said. 'I know, Miri. You'll be good for him, I can feel it.'

———————————

On the weekend, Liss's sisters arrived on the two o'clock ferry. 'Tash, May,' Liss said, squeezing my arm, 'this is Miri, Mickey's girlfriend.' And now I could hear them in the kitchen, singing 'Video Killed the Radio Star'.

'Miri, come join us!'

They were playing dirty Scrabble, their own perverse version of the game, but I knew I couldn't compete with them. They were inventive and endlessly obscene.

'Miri!' Liss called again.

I was lying in bed. Even with the door closed, I could still hear them. Structurally, the cottage seemed thin, insubstantial, constructed of paper and sticks.

Tash's voice was the loudest. My mother would call her a pistol. A tawny, nervy girl. 'Where's Sal going to sleep tonight, if we're staying in your room?'

'He can sleep on the sofa.'

'Mr Right,' May said.

'Mr Right Now,' Liss said.

'Gallant,' Tash said.

'Listen, Mickey, I'm here to help you,' Sal said the night he showed up at the cousins' little yellow house on Pillette Road. Mickey had a futon in the damp basement, where we watched *Atom Age Vampire* and drank Orange Crush from milk-glass mugs with *Beautiful Ontario, Canada* on the side.

'I guess there's a first time for everything,' Mickey said. He hadn't let his brother turn on the lights in the basement, so we all sat in the dark, Sal's face lit ghoulishly by the television screen, the movie still playing. *You are nothing if not mine*, the scientist said.

What Sal wanted was for Mickey to come and work with him. He had heard from the cousins that Mickey had quit his last job working for a graffiti-removal company, power-washing obscenities off concrete and brick.

'Work with you,' Mickey scoffed. Sal had recently become the manager of a motel. He said he had jobs for both of us, if we wanted. The Blue Haven. 'That place is a dump.'

'We've been fixing it up.'

'I have other career options.'

'Oh, yeah?'

'Sure. I was thinking of getting my real estate license.'

Sal leaned back and laughed. 'Yeah? You think it's just that easy? And who's gonna want to buy a house from someone like you? You look like a suspect in a police sketch. Come on, Mickey. What have you got to lose?' And at this Sal waved a hand around the damp basement. 'All this you got here, yeah. I know. How could you leave all this?' The drooping futon, the leaking ceiling, the spiders, the drippy-eyed paintings of clowns on black velvet. I felt myself included in the dismissive sweep of Sal's hand. 'Is this about Liss?'

'That girl is dead to me.'

Sal folded his hands together, kept them there as if he were praying. 'Perfect. So you have no reason not to. Meet me in Leamington at the dock, Monday at noon. Bring your girlfriend.'

———————————

Now here we were. Mickey had gone somewhere without telling me—he never did say where he was going, or when he would come back. I ventured into the kitchen. Liss and her sisters were sitting on the counters. Liss slid to the side, tapped the place beside her, then poured me a drink. I climbed up. Tash had done everyone's makeup. Her eyelids glittered with rose gold. May shone with silver eyeliner. Liss was wearing matte lipstick the dark pinkish colour of butcher paper.

'Who won Scrabble?' I asked.

'Liss,' May said. 'By like a hundred points.'

Tash said, 'She has a very good vocabulary.'

Liss got the bottle of gin and the yellow plastic pitcher full of lemonade and mixed us all more drinks in white Pyrex coffee cups with green daisies all around the rim.

'How do you want me to do your eye makeup?' Tash asked her.

'Purple,' she said, licking the knife she used to stir the drinks. 'Like a smoky-eyed look.'

Tash opened her makeup bag, removed compacts of pressed powder—lavender, lilac—eyeliner, mascara, a yellow cream she called primer, which she daubed on her sister's eyelids to start.

The lemonade was from a powder mix, and when I finished my drink, there was a sugary grit at the bottom of my cup.

'Do you want me to do your makeup, too?' Tash asked.

The name is misleading; there are no vampires in *Atom Age Vampire*. Instead it is about a starlet, Jeanette, disfigured by a car wreck, and a scientist who will do anything to save her.

('No, not to save her,' Liss said one time. She had seen the movie too, with blonde Jeanette in a fur coat drawn up over her mouth, hiding bruises behind sunglasses in the aftermath of her car crash. The scientist blamed Jeanette for all his crimes, said she made him a monster. *You can never understand what it has cost me.* 'Just to restore her beauty. He thinks that's saving her.')

'All right,' I said. 'Sure. Thank you.'

'What do you want?'

'I don't know.'

'Do a cat's eye,' Liss said. 'Here.' She took a stick of eyeliner, warmed the tip between her lips before passing it to Tash. 'Now it'll go on more smoothly.'

At the Blue Haven, Mickey did maintenance and groundskeeping, which meant he spent a lot of time in the field behind the motel getting high. Sal wouldn't let him work at the desk, or handle any customer service directly. 'First of all, you're fucked up all the time,' he said, 'and even if you were sober, you're too twitchy and weird. You'd give people a Norman Bates vibe.'

Liss agreed. 'You've got this dark energy now,' she murmured, touching her hand to his cheek. He swatted her away.

'Don't touch me.'

Another time I heard them talking outside our bedroom window, first Liss's voice rising above the insect drone of the field. 'How are you today?'

'Leave me alone.'

'Mickey, it doesn't have to be this way—'

The screen door smacked shut. Mickey appeared in our bedroom, his curls even darker with sweat. 'I knew this was a mistake.' He worked his way out of his damp Nirvana t-shirt, his body thin and pale as dead coral.

'So why don't we go?'

Mickey lay down on the bed beside me, smell of hard liquor sweating out. His blue eyes were bloodshot. 'Go where?' Mickey said. 'And do what?'

I put a hesitant hand on his shoulder. 'I thought you said you were thinking of a real estate license.' For a moment I could even imagine it: Mickey in a nice button-up shirt, with business cards and everything.

'I just said that so Sal would knock it off,' he said. 'And anyway, he was right. I could never do that. Like, you'd have to know about property law and mortgages and shit.'

'I bet you could learn.'

'No,' he said, staring at the peeling wallpaper. 'I can't.'

'I'd help you study.'

'Miri,' he said, 'that's really nice of you. But it's not going to happen.' He rolled away from me, buried his face in his pillow. 'I think I need to go to sleep for awhile.'

———————

Sal had said to Liss, 'I can give you anything you want.' I couldn't imagine saying that to someone. I couldn't imagine believing in the ability—to give it, or receive it. *Anything you want* was a trap. You were supposed to know this, from fairy tales. No wish is granted without a secret catch.

We wore white starched aprons tied around our waists. There were seven rooms at the motel altogether. We were supposed to dust everything, even the lampshades and picture frames, but Liss said we didn't have to bother. The light was usually so dim in the rooms, who could ever tell anyway? The mirrors in the rooms were all shrouded with clouds. At first I tried to scrub them clean, but Liss said there wasn't any point. The silver backing was tarnished; the summers were too humid here.

In the last room that morning, we found a little row of shells and stones left on the windowsill. Liss turned them over, one by one. She held up a grey oval stone. 'It's a fossil,' she said. 'You should bring this to Mickey.'

'Yeah?'

She nodded. 'He used to be really into this kind of stuff. Fossils, dinosaurs. When we were kids he wanted to be a palaeontologist. We used to watch *The Land Before Time* like, every day. I remember one morning he told me he'd found bones—he dug for hours. They were just the roots of trees. But he really believed it.'

'Oh,' I said. 'He never told me.'

'Really? Well. It was years ago, I guess.'

'He never told me about you, either.' It was a mean thing to say, but Liss only shrugged, dreamy and serene.

'What we had was kind of intense,' she said. 'It would've been a lot to explain to a girl he had just met. Really heavy.' She passed me the stone. 'It looks like teeth—maybe part of a jawbone. He'll be so excited.'

'All right.' I dropped the stone in the pocket of my apron. I hadn't seen Mickey even mildly excited about anything since we'd come here. Maybe even a long time before that.

The room done, we walked out into the sunlight. The stone smacked against my thigh. A little flock of mourning doves watched us from the telephone wire, cooing gloomily. 'Liss!' a woman wearing mushroom-coloured khaki and a pair of binoculars called out. Liss was not the most dutiful maid, but the guests loved her, and she loved them too. I left her by the picnic table, listening to a pair of birdwatchers tell her about the sandhill crane they'd seen at Lighthouse Point.

I found Mickey sitting on a bleached piece of driftwood under the hoptrees. The beach across the road from the motel was just a skinny strip of stony sand. I slid my fingers over the stone in my apron and sat down beside him.

His eyes were closed. The sun was gold across his face. I knew he was supposed to be mowing the lawn that morning. 'What are you doing?'

'Just waiting for everything to kick in.'

I nodded. The lake sloshed up over the stones. If you crushed the hoptree leaves between your fingers, they left a citrus tang.

'You should come with me sometime,' he said.

'Where?' I asked, hopeful for a moment. He slid an Altoids tin from the pocket of his jeans. He shook it. I heard a dry rattle of pills.

'Maybe another time,' I said. I knew I couldn't; I would like it too much. I would never come back. In the pocket of my apron the stone weighed me down.

'All right,' Mickey said. He stood up, brushing sand from his jeans. 'I'm gonna go lie down.'

Leave me alone, Mickey still said when Liss tried to talk to him, but now he also said *please*. My hands smelled like bleach. *Please leave me alone.* Maybe love was never symbiotic, like I'd wanted to believe. Maybe it was only ever a form of parasitism.

A few feet away, a yellow perch lay on the beach, scales flaking off, beaded with insects. The hoptree leaves flickered with sunlight. The lake was as cloudy as the motel mirrors. If you looked in them quickly, it was like seeing ghosts. I drew the stone from my apron, held the smooth grey oval in the palm of my hand, weighing it. There was a piece of fossilized sea coral on our dresser the other day. Mickey must have brought it in from the beach. Or maybe Liss had left it there, a subsidy of guilt, a gift. I threw the stone into the lake. It sank glumly. Sunlight glittered like sequins on the water.

'We are mermaids,' Liss said. But people always forget that mermaids are monsters.

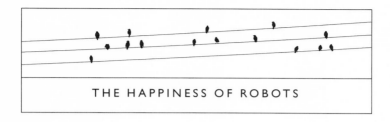

THE HAPPINESS OF ROBOTS

We were iridescent with sweat, haloed with the August heat. I said we should go swimming in the lake, but Cady said Elio didn't know how. Instead we had to burn.

Elio said, 'I can just watch you.'

'No,' Cady said, peeling the skirt of her white eyelet dress away from her skin. Her eyes glimmered, distant and feverish. 'That wouldn't be right.'

We stood at the side of the cottage, in the garden of mint and pennyroyal, full of drowsy bees and a few pale cabbage butterflies with wings the same dusty white as Cady's summer dress. On the lawn by the road was a sign: *A Place in the Sun*. 'What a depressing name for a cottage,' I said. 'It feels like bad luck.'

Cady wiped at the perspiration across her forehead, shining like a tiara. 'It sounds good, I guess.'

Elio's Nirvana t-shirt was dark with sweat, damp across his chest. 'What the hell are you two talking about?'

'*A Place in the Sun* was a movie,' Cady said.

'Never heard of it.'

I knew that he wouldn't catch the reference, and I was secretly pleased whenever he didn't understand something between Cady and me. 'I guess no one remembers,' I said, 'what happened to the girl, in the end.' But Cady wasn't listening. It wasn't even noon yet. The trees drooped, dripping green against the white sky. She was standing there, by Elio's side, her gaze somewhere across the road, towards the holographic shimmer of sunlight on water and sky. The sunshine was so bright that it left a corona of light around her head, like the auras that beamed around stars and moons.

Sun in my eyes and the salt drip of sweat, wet all down my neck. ───────────────

In the afternoons, before he joined us, Cady would try calling Elio on her cell phone, despite the weak reception. Cady shipwrecked on the island, Elio on the mainland—set asunder by Lake Erie. The separation was romantic. I watched her try to languish for him, although pining away was not as easy as it seemed in those Victorian novels. Cady was no wan heroine—she wore the gold shimmer of summer all over her. She had been the star sweeper of our soccer team, and when she ran full out, no one could catch her. Still, Cady sighed, gazed across the water, kept a tally of the days till she and Elio would meet again. At night, in the small room we shared, I lay in my twin bed beside her and listened to the lake lap at the shore across the road as Cady relived her summer with Elio: the late night car rides with the radio on; the wedding where they had danced all night; the three times he'd taken her to the movie theatre at Devonshire Mall so they could watch *The Notebook* (he had cried, secretly, in the dark beside her); the nights in her backyard trying to name all the constellations....

During the days, while Cady circled the lawn, cell phone clamped against her ear in hopes of hearing from Elio, I sat in the living room, making my way through a damp volume of *Funk & Wagnalls Standard Dictionary*, page by page. (*Hope: 1. To desire with expectation of fulfillment; I hope to be able to join you. 2. To wish; want: I hope that you will be happy.*) It was one volume of a set of two; the second was missing, but *A through Lobar* was still a worthy summer goal. It would be a prudent use of time, preparation for September, when Cady and I started university, maybe, finally, leaving Elio behind.

───────────────

Elio wasn't supposed to be on the island with us at all.

'It's a family vacation,' Cady's mother, Rita, had said, but she finally relented, after weeks of Cady imploring her. Elio could come for the last weekend of vacation, a compromise which satisfied no one—not Cady, who wanted him there the whole time and not Rita, who didn't want him at all.

We got to the dock to meet Elio just as the ferry passengers disembarked. While Cady waited, I hid in the washroom of the restaurant across the road, deep breathing over the sink. When I finally came out, Elio and Cady were standing in the waning crowd, his arm around her waist, his face against her throat. 'Hey,' he said, without looking up. When Elio and I had dated, he'd been growing this strange, sparse beard, but now the smooth line of his new jaw was startling. 'I made him shave it off,' Cady told me once. I pressed my palms against my dress, a mirror image of Cady's. We'd been drawn to the same one at the mall last spring and had bought two—in different shades so we could trade, Cady said. ('Do you share everything?' Elio had asked, and I'd said, 'Of course not.')

'Hey, Elio. Nice to see you again.'

He made this low sound, a laugh or a growl, still pressed against her throat. But Cady was looking at him now, at the bluish ink on his forearm—a small galaxy of stars, which he'd done himself at sixteen with a safety pin. 'Your tattoo. You have to cover it.'

'With what?'

'Like a sweater or something…'

'It's going to be in the eighties all weekend. I didn't bring any sweaters with me.'

'You can't let my mom see. She can't stand tattoos.'

'Your mom already hates me anyway. I haven't seen you for a week. Why don't we go across the street? We can all have a drink together.'

— 181 —

('We have these totally random things in common,' Cady had said, that night, months ago, when she'd told me her feelings for Elio. 'We know all the same words to all the same songs ...') But now Cady was frowning, her thumb rubbing the ink like she could wipe it away. 'No drinking this weekend. You're supposed to be trying to get my parents to like you. Besides, they won't serve us.'

'I'm nineteen.'

'We're seventeen.'

'Clem has a fake ID. We'll buy you your drinks.'

Cady frowned. 'I'm going to the clinic. Maybe they have some bandages or something we can use.' We watched Cady cross the road to the lawn of the clinic, which looked like a yellow-painted house behind the Municipal Building, an ambulance parked in the gravel driveway.

'What about you, Clementine? You want to join me for a drink?'

'Cady said no.'

'Remember the time we got so drunk on gin? They kicked you out of the bar for throwing up in a urinal.'

'I don't remember.' He'd held my hair when I stopped on the walk home to get sick in the bushes. You don't forget things like that. Or how he used to sing all the words to 'My Darling Clementine', sounding like Yukon Cornelius.

'You still like gin? I'll buy you a drink.'

('We're not right together,' I had said, and he said, 'I'm not right for you, is what you mean.' I reminded myself it was true.) 'No thanks.'

'Come on. Don't you want one? I know you, Clementine. We used to tell each other everything.'

Now Cady was back, with a roll of cotton gauze. 'They let me have this, after I begged them. I said it was for my dog. You should thank me.'

Elio held out his arm. 'I will.'

Cady unrolled the gauze and then wrapped it around and around his arm, her hands steady, perfect. 'There,' she said, examining her work. 'That looks better. You can say you burnt your arm on something.'

We met first, at a party. A motel on Huron Church Road. Through the windows of the room you could see the Ambassador Bridge. The Skyview Motel.

'Doesn't every motel have a view of the sky?' Elio had asked.

'I believe in setting the bar low.'

'So that's why you're talking to me.'

'No—'

'It's okay. It's only a joke.'

It was the start—of his double-edged questions, of my wrong answers. I had come with my cousin Charlotte, and she had disappeared with some other girls down the hallway. Elio had been standing there alone, awkwardly as me. The air conditioner was broken and the curtains had been drawn, hopelessly, against the heat. The asphalt outside the window glittered beneath the sunset. Elio's face was damp in the late August swelter; he kept tugging his shirt, uselessly, separating it from his clammy chest.

'I think this is blood on the carpet.'

'Probably,' Elio agreed, stepping aside. I'd borrowed a pair of Charlotte's kitten heels, two sizes too small, and I wanted so badly to sit down, but there was only the bed. After we started dating, we used to sit in parking lots with the radio on and talk so much we missed the movies we had gone to see, drift on the swings in the park, until the stars punctured the sky. We'd go to Bulk Barn for bags of cinnamon hearts that burnt our mouths, our lips red as candy. *My Darling Clementine.*

But by November, I was drowning in his blue and wild moods. I waited until after his birthday, an entire week. 'You knew this was coming,' he had said when we broke up, and of course it was true, I had. For months afterwards, until Cady—and even after that, once or twice, he would call, saying I had ruined everything. It felt unfair but also intoxicating, to have the power to ruin something, even if I didn't believe in it.

———————

The next day we walked back from the Pelee Island lighthouse, last lit in 1909. With pockets full of beach glass, we made our way through the woods, back to the road. Just Cady and me; 'I hate walking,' Elio said. 'I'll stay here and wait for you.'

'Elio told me he had a dream about you last week.'

'Yeah?' I had gone to bed early, leaving Elio and Cady on the front porch. He had brought his guitar. 'I can show you how to play "Polly",' he'd offered, but the thought made me sick. *E minor G D C E minor.* Elio's hands over Cady's as he showed her the chords. Or over mine. Either way, I had to leave.

Cady stopped by the side of the road. Trying not to smile. 'He said, "I had a dream Clementine drowned."'

'I guess I won't go in the water.'

'He said he woke up disappointed.' Now she was smiling. 'Clementine! Come on. Elio was just joking around. You know how he is.'

'I should know, I guess.'

('I'm finally so happy, Clem,' Cady confessed, weeks earlier. She was lit up with love, a star going supernova. Jealousy was a vulture on my chest, eating my heart out, breaking open my ribs.)

'I'm done. I won't talk about him anymore. It's too weird.'

'You can talk to me about him,' I said. 'You can talk to me about anything.'

'No,' Cady said. 'It's bothering you. That's why you went to bed early last night.'

'I just wanted to go to sleep.'

'Do you ever just get so tired of being fake all the time? Because you're not even a good actress. It must be so exhausting.'

Cady was right and I knew it. It was my secret fear, that everything about me was actually fake. Acrylic nails over my real ones, my dyed hair, the extra padding I slipped in my bra. The other things, too—the way I smiled when I didn't mean it or said yes when I wanted to say no. I lied all the time like that. The prospect of really being myself was terrifying.

———————

Sunday evening, things fell apart because Elio wouldn't play Scrabble. *Cape Fear* was on the television, Robert Mitchum drawling, *Ah now, come on.* Cady and Elio had just returned from a walk along the beach. I sat on the living room floor, sorting our beach glass. It was soothing. Maybe all my life could be divided into tidy little jobs. I would be happy in the metallic way robots are—coded, contented, autonomous.

'You're supposed to be trying to make a good impression on my parents.' Cady's mascara had a drippy look to it, black underneath her eyes, like the fierce, jilted girls of Lichtenstein's pop art.

'Well, I won't if I play Scrabble. I'm a really bad speller.'

'You don't even want to try.'

'Seriously, Cady, I suck. Ask Clementine.'

The beach glass clinked into the jars. 'It's kind of true,' I said, finally. 'He can never use the right form of *their*. Or *too*.'

'It's why Clementine broke up with me,' Elio said, and I laughed, but shouldn't have.

'You're not as funny as you think you are,' Cady said, before she left the room. In the kitchen I could hear the scatter of Scrabble tiles across the board. I dropped green glass into a jar and tried not to look at Elio. Not at him, and not at the faint trace of mascara on his cheek, just below his eye.

Our memories are redacted. How can I say now if, when I left, I wanted him to follow me? There is some relief in that, in not knowing anymore. Years later I realized I always drank to the point where all became automatic, my body mechanical, thoughts robotic, synapses shotgunned.

Behind the cottage the woods met you, suddenly—dark skein of brush and then the trees. Damp smell of leaves and dirt after the rain. Ten feet in, I stopped, sat on a fallen tree—shellbark.

'Hey.' There was Elio, sweating already when he sat down beside me. 'What are you doing here?' Named by his mother for Eliodoro Lombardi, nineteenth-century Italian poet—Elio, who hated to read and hadn't touched a book since coerced by high school teachers. *El-io-doro*, how Cady said his full name sometimes, the way I hated, slowly and dragged out, like she had a mouthful of sticky candy.

'Good question,' I said. 'Existential.' His hand disappeared into the pocket of his grunge jeans, to his mickey of gin. On his arm, the bandages hiding his tattoo were beginning to come undone. In grade two my class had conducted a science experiment: sink or float. We'd dropped whatever we could find in an aquarium—bark, stones, pinecones. We were all like the objects in that experiment. Some of us were born buoyant, others doomed to sink due to elements and circumstances out of our hands—and in them, sometimes, too.

Elio drank first, then let me have a turn. I immediately felt its warm efflorescence in my chest. ('I just want you to be happy,' I'd said when we broke up, and he'd said, 'Why can't we be happy together?')

'You're drunk,' I said.

'Admit it, you like me better this way.' But I wasn't sure if I liked him at all, most of the time. I used to feel I would die if he touched me and now I felt I would die if he didn't. I tried not to think about

Cady, the pictures we took, crushed together to take in the photo booth at Devonshire Mall, Cady's cursive on the back, *love you like a sister*. I tried not to think about our sleepovers—we watched horror movies and were so afraid of ghosts but I always said I wasn't. I pretended like I held Cady's hand across the span of our sleeping bags for her sake and not mine, too.

The years alter memory like a prism alters light, fracturing it the way the branches of the trees above broke the last sunlight into pieces, until all that's left is broken. All that remains: hands to hips, *don't stop* instead of *don't, stop*, the green leaves, the damp woods, the wet dirt. Cady. Her ankles tender with insect bites. She wore her blue soccer socks to sleep because her feet were always cold. She'd found me three days ago reading on the beach, stopped talking mid-sentence: 'Oh, here I am talking to you when you're almost done your book. When someone does that to me I feel like it's the end of the world.'

I stood up. In the trees over us you could hear the yellow warblers—*sweet, sweet, I'm so sweet*, in the hickory and ash. 'This never happened.'

He stood up too. 'Cady said she told you, that dream I had.'

'You dreamed I drowned.' Walking away, towards the cottage. 'But you can't even swim.'

Inside, Cady and her family were still playing Scrabble. The dim light from the kitchen pooled on the dark living room floor, oil floating on water. It was too late to join them. The television was on, gloomy luminosity of black and white. Robert Mitchum, sweating, swaggering, cracked his knuckles. Not Gregory Peck—good, lawful, and clean—who my heart beat for, full of sympathy and love, but Robert Mitchum instead. Criminal and imminent, a convict cumulating rage, calculating the grim arithmetic of loss.

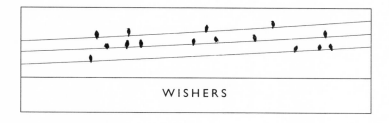

WISHERS

'Go now, Persephone, to your dark-robed mother, go, and feel kindly in your heart towards me: be not so exceedingly cast down; for I shall be no unfitting husband for you among the deathless gods.' —Homer, *Hymn to Demeter*

I went as far as I could before I got to the water, and then I stopped. A lakeside town in winter. In this season the population dropped, the streets went to sleep. The trees bared their spines, and the watercolour-tinted cottages along the lake shut their doors till summertime. At Point Pelee, the birders appeared to observe the Arctic breeding birds that had come south for the winter: the longspurs and buntings, various types of ducks, the redpolls, tiny finches with red caps, almost elfin, pipits, the little songbirds, that I had before come to see, with Cora. She had stood on the frozen beach in her pale green wool scarf, her face turned to the sky; I remember that she had looked so happy, then, and I had believed she was.

Once every ten years the temperature crept low enough for Lake Erie to freeze. A cold snap this past weekend had left an American freighter trapped in the lake for days. They had to send the coast guard out to break up the ice, to clear the way for shipments of coal and grain.

I parked my car in the motel lot, at the far end where the pavement crumbled into gravel, and I sat there with the door open, waiting. Waiting, but for what sign? Her face at a window? That murky feeling, maternal instinct, to guide my way? That was nothing but oxytocin, a chemical lie seeping from the hypothalamus, poisoning the blood. The love drug. I closed the car door, kept my keys in my hand, buttoned my dark coat. Cora had called me that morning and told me she'd been staying here. Or the voice on the other line had said she was Cora, but she didn't sound the same. 'How long have you been living there?' I asked, and Cora said, 'I don't remember,' her voice sleepy, vague. *How can you not remember*, I wanted to ask, *you, a girl who kept a colour-coded calendar, meticulous notes in her field journal, who once organized my spice cabinet alphabetically ... allspice, anise, basil, bay leaf, bird's-eye chili.* Now I could hear Hayes in the background: *Come on, let's go, I'm ready.* 'Where are you going?' I asked, but the line went dead.

You could feel the teeth of the breeze, see the dark scratch of trees along the long white wrist of the sky. February weather. It was a month of ice and mud.

Tomorrow would be Valentine's Day. I read once of a place, in Italy somewhere, where lovers exchanged keys, tokens meant to unlock the heart. The lock-and-key motif seemed a more fitting symbol for the story of a jailed martyr than the paper hearts, the red roses, the candied gestures of affection swapped here. And then I remembered the bridge in Paris, the Pont des Arts. Lovers left padlocks all along the railings and threw the keys into the Seine as a sign of their commitment. Or at least they did, until part of the bridge collapsed, burdened by the weight of all that love.

There's a Slovenian proverb from a book of folklore: *Saint Valentine brings the keys of roots*, suggesting the day marks the moment when the first green tendrils of spring would stretch, uncurl from their sleep in the earth and creep out into the light to bloom. There didn't seem to be any sign of that now. You could see the grass dried dark as burned hair and matted to the ground wherever the crusted snow had broken. Behind the two-storey white building was the lake, the beach scrolled with frozen foam. The building was called the Meadows now. It used to be the Lakeview, years ago. Just off the highway. The motel had a motto: *You're only a stranger once.*

'Don't never leave me,' my daughter said, when she was three or four. She used to say things like that. 'What happens one day if I just kept walking and walking and never came home? What happens when we are far away?'

'Far away from what?' I asked. She had questions I couldn't answer.

'What happens if I'm not here?' she asked. 'What happens if I'm nowhere?'

'What do you mean, nowhere?'

'Like if I'm lost,' she said, leaving me with an uneasy feeling even as I reassured her, 'No, no, that won't happen, ever.' One of those little lies we whisper to children. Do we damage our children with our small dishonesties? Did I leave Cora unprepared? Should I have taken her by the hand and walked her through the shadows, instead of pretending there was only sunshine? Too late now. At nineteen, she had gone on without me.

When she was a baby, she'd been allergic to peanut butter. The doctor told me to dose her with a small dab every day so that her tolerance could build up, so that one day she'd be immune. And now I wonder if pain should be prescribed the same way, a little at a time, so that we are not so stunned by it.

When she was young, Cora slept with me at night, her face pressed so close to mine that some mornings there was a faint lashing of mascara on her cheek. I remember her picking things in the garden, even in the winter—the flowers dry and dead, petals sticking to her mittens. Her favourite toy was her medical kit: a pretend blood pressure cuff, a spring-loaded syringe, a plastic stethoscope she wore round her neck. 'Hello, my heart,' she'd say, as she listened. She could have been a doctor. She could have been anything.

What dreams we have for our children; how aggrieved we are when they dare deviate.

She was a biology student when she disappeared. Nineteen, in her second year of university. Her heart belonged to herpetology, the study of reptiles and amphibians—creeping animals. Her passion was snakes. Her bedroom was a library, full of scientific journals: *Bibliotheca Herpetologica, Copeia,* and *Chelonian Conservation and Biology: International Journal of Turtle and Tortoise Research.* Labelled illustrations of snake skeletons decorated the walls, and she pressed loose articles torn from newspapers and magazines in between dusty encyclopedias before tucking them into the frame of her mirror. They were notes for the paper she was writing: *An Examination of the Maternal Instinct in Snakes.*

'I thought they laid their eggs and left them,' I said.

Cora shook her head. 'No, no, that's only some species. Anyway, first you have to consider your conception of maternal love,' she said. 'The act of nest building itself is a gesture of love. As is incubation. Timber rattlesnakes have shown the ability to recognize their siblings. And some Eastern Massasauga rattlesnakes have been observed wrapping their bodies around their neonates to guard them from danger.'

She felt called to the field of ecology, called to the rescue of her first true love, the Massasauga rattlesnake. Misunderstood, she told me, abused, killed from fear, sadly listed as a Species at Risk in Ontario. There were two main populations. The Great Lakes and Saint Lawrence population was threatened, but ours—the Carolinian population—was considered more gravely endangered. It was the only venomous snake in Ontario. 'Only known to bite in self-defence,' Cora said. It had cat-like pupils, a sturdy body, and it was equipped with a cytotoxic venom. Known by other names—black snapper, muck rattler, swamp rattlesnake. Of all the creatures, Cora chose to devote herself to this one, to the cause of restoring its populations along the shores of the Great Lakes. It was understandable; her heart was susceptible to all maligned creatures.

After she was gone, my friends warned me she might never again be the person she was when she left. 'Who do you want to come home, Demetria?' they asked. 'Are you only looking for the Cora you knew? Are you ready to accept who she might be now?' As if, like a bird whose fledgling had been returned to the nest, I'd smell the predator on her feathers, refuse her absolutely. But I was ready; I was waiting. I would know her anywhere, in any way. I would bring her home again.

———————

The first time Hayes came to dinner was the last time. Cora and I spent the afternoon before his arrival baking a cake. Lemon chiffon, with yellow curlicues of rind grated over vanilla frosting. The recipe asked for seven eggs, separated. Cora had whisked the yolks in a blue bowl, lemon stuck to her fingers, while I measured the flour, baking powder, sugar, and salt. The doorbell rang and she looked at me, but I couldn't translate the expression on her face. She had been restless all day. Her dark hair was in a braided crown, done that morning in anticipation of tonight's dinner; it was coming loose now, long strands unweaving themselves. She wore a long white halter dress with lace that went around her neck. Her eye makeup was smoky, gold at the edges, and her matte lipstick was so dark it was almost purple. She had pierced her ears over and over through her earlier teenage years—three rhinestones along the side in each lobe, a slim silver hoop through the curve of cartilage at the top.

('Why do you let her mutilate herself like that?' her father had asked, and I told him, 'It's her decision; her body is not just an extension of ours.' Her father, with all his other loves before, during, and after our marriage, considered himself a moral authority. But men like that always do.)

Cora's piercings glittered, small fixed points of light, like constellations in the night sky.

'Aren't you going to answer the door?' I asked.

'No, no, you do it,' she said, straightening her long skirt, twisting her bracelet round her wrist, a gold bangle with a raw amethyst, looking anywhere but at the door.

When I opened the door, Hayes stood there on the other side, smiling. 'Welcome,' I said, and his smile sharpened at the edges like he sensed he wasn't. Cora had implored me, though, days after she met him, to try, to get to know him, and so here he was, holding a bouquet of roses and violets and crocuses with their open yellow throats.

'Thank you for having me,' he said as he stepped in, his gaze already searching for her, but Cora had disappeared into the kitchen. I hoped she would stay there. He removed his dark overcoat and I caught the glint of his stainless steel watch — Swiss, numberless, just a small dark face with two silver hands. The scent of his cologne: cardamom milk and cypress trees.

We took our places at the table, Cora at his side, myself across from him, the flowers between us, in a vase my own mother had brought here from Italy, painted with coiling red foliage, the old glaze flaking. I served the first course, eggplant *caponata*; the black olives shone like little eyes. At first we ate in silence, besides Hayes's murmured, 'My compliments, Demetria. This is even better than the food at the wedding.' I couldn't bring myself to thank him, so I gave a cursory nod and said nothing, despite Cora's reproachful gaze.

I served *insalata di frutti di mare*, listening as Cora and Hayes finally began to converse. 'Fruit of the sea, if my inadequate Italian serves,' he said, and she smiled, nodded *yes, yes*. She spoke of the salad, the spices required — the lemon juice, the bay leaves, the oregano, the parsley. How she had gone to La Stella on Erie Street to get the freshest octopus, shrimp, and squid. How you wanted dry-packed scallops, not the ones that had been soaking in brine, and he said she should show him, she should bring him one day, because to him all deep-sea suckered things looked the same. He said he loved how she didn't squirm.

But why should she, a budding field biologist? She spent her summers bicycling down dirt roads to record incidents of reptile road mortality, counting snakes at Massasauga gestation sites. She'd showed me the thin, stainless steel snake hooks they used to safely capture and release the specimens they sought. She held all kinds of reptiles, fed them insects with bare hands.

'You know about me,' Cora said, 'but I don't know about you,' and Hayes smiled, shrugged. 'What is there to know?' He had three sisters and two brothers. He was the estranged son of a wealthy family, but he had been cut off from the family business, Marram Brothers Funeral Homes, with locations throughout Essex County. He shrugged, briefly smiled. Why should he care? Who wanted to be king of the dead, anyway? 'I am the unseen one,' he said. He said that he had knowledge of noble things, but no good use for it, and Cora nodded, blooming with sympathy, sweet as small spring flowers. Suddenly, he put down his glass. His smile shrank, his white teeth eclipsed by his lips. A year before he had been in a terrible accident, he said. He had been on the highway. Blunt force trauma broke his ribs, fractured vertebrae. He had scars from shattered glass. Nerve damage that would never fully heal. Facial numbness. *I was dead*, he said. But at the hospital, they brought him back—to life, but not consciousness, not right away. He awoke seventeen days later, alone, writhing in pain. Cora, her eyes glittering, wiped shining tears on the backs of her hands.

After dinner, I went into the kitchen to get the cake. As I stood at the counter, sliding slices onto bone china plates, I grew aware of a shift in the shadows, and when I turned, Hayes was standing there, a few feet behind me. His face was calm, still as a sculpture. I could smell the clean cypress green of his cologne. 'I came to thank you, Mama, for inviting me to dinner,' and I said, 'Don't call me that.' His gaze went to the knife still in my hand, and he smiled. 'Let

— 195 —

go of your anger,' he said, 'all your helpless rage. I'll be no unfitting husband for your daughter.'

———————————

They met at a wedding at the art gallery, where my restaurant catered events. Sun Parlour Café was the restaurant's name, taken from a 1912 book—*Essex County, the Sun Parlour of Canada: Opportunities for Farming and Gardening*. A place described by the Toronto *Globe* in 1900 as 'Eden without the serpent', a description that stung Cora.

On the weekends, Cora worked as a banquet server at the weddings while I supervised the kitchen. She dressed like all the other waitresses, in a dark skirt and neat white blouse buttoned up, hair pulled back into a ponytail. Her pierced ears shone in the candlelight. Back and forth she went, bringing small dishes of almond milk pudding speckled with cinnamon and candied orange peel, the last course. *Biancomangiare*, my mother called it. I made my own almond milk. Cora had helped me peel the almonds, measure out the orange blossom water.

'O sole mio' was playing, a sweeping song, slow, operatic. *My sunshine*. I saw him standing by the windows overlooking the river, a dark silhouette against the Detroit skyline shining in the water below. Suit jacket open over a white button-down shirt, pale pocket square folded neatly, the gleam of a stainless steel watch on his wrist. His dark hair was shaved short at the sides then brushed back at the top, and his cool mouth was filled with perfect teeth—expensive orthodontia, no doubt. Everything about him was precise and clean. He had his gaze locked on Cora, tracking her, barely moving, as she crossed the dance floor carrying trays of glasses wadded with crushed napkins. A hawk on a telephone wire watching a rabbit in the grass.

I waited till Cora had gone up the stairs to serve drinks and collect empty bottles from amongst the guests who wandered the gallery halls, gazing at paintings and dancing close to the stars. At those gallery weddings, guests could float between the floors, studying the landscapes of the Group of Seven, those gloomy love songs to northern lakes, windswept pines. 'Can I help you?' I asked him, standing close enough to feel the hot scotch on his breath. I realized suddenly I had seen him here another time, two weeks before, at a party for a yacht club. He'd been wearing a maroon suit jacket and a sky-blue pocket square bordered in the same shade as the jacket, like it had been dipped in claret, or blood. I knew then that he wasn't a guest at this wedding, that he had come back for Cora.

'I need her,' he said.

'Pardon me?'

'You heard me,' he murmured.

'Go to hell.'

He looked at me, blue eyes under a sweep of long lashes. His half-moon smile, the waxing crescent of his teeth. 'Where do you think I came from, Mama?' he whispered, leaning in close enough for me to feel his heat against my cheek. 'I'll go. But I'm waiting for her.'

———————————

I remember the first night she came home late. Cora, always punctual, precise to the point that any lateness pained her. 'Where were you?' I asked. I'd been sitting in the dark living room, the television on. A vampire movie—Dracula, his gaze lowered for a moment, long lashes against waxen cheekbones, fangs demurely tucked behind closed lips. *Love, I mean no harm.* But harm that isn't meant is felt all the same.

'I was at the library.' She walked into the kitchen, keeping the lights off. She wore a white cardigan open over her dress—light blue, with a rose gold floral print that shimmered, like the dust on a butterfly's wings. 'Scales,' Cora had told me. 'Not dust.' In the fall she had planted milkweed for the monarchs, and the crisper drawer had been full of cold-stratified seeds waiting for the sun. Now she moved on through the shadows. Her perfume smelled of roses on the cusp of decay. Her dark hair shone slick as blood.

'You didn't come home with any books? I've never seen you come home from the library without a whole stack of books in your arms.'

'People change,' Cora said.

But she was wrong. Time shifts us, erodes us, but the bones it reveals were always part of us.

———————

She disappeared at the end of August. It was the Tecumseh Corn Festival. She'd asked me to pick her up at midnight, but when I went to the park she was gone. Her friends, a clueless crew in cut-offs and flower crowns, had no idea where she was. They stood in a loose group, diaphanous as fish flies, texting, scrolling through their phones. 'She was just here,' they said. 'With Hayes.'

Across the field, grass matted down with the grease and oil of carnival machinery, the Ferris wheel continued its giddy rotation. The summer air was humid, sticky with the smell of cotton candy. I imagined Cora with him, somewhere I couldn't follow.

———————

In October, Kate called me from Devonshire Mall. She had seen Cora there, she said, with Hayes. I went right away, but it was too late. They were gone.

'Where did you see her?'

Kate held her hand out. 'Here,' she said. 'The food court.' Illuminated by wide skylights, it was so bright I could barely see. It seemed impossible that after months, Cora could resurface here, in the most mundane of places.

'How was she?' I asked. 'What did she look like?'

Kate hesitated. She hadn't spoken to her, she said. She looked different. At first she almost hadn't recognized her. Then she took off her glasses.

'Cora doesn't wear glasses.'

'Sunglasses,' Kate said, 'a pair of aviators—gold rims, blue shades. Beautiful.'

She was wearing grey sweatpants, a green army jacket. Black boots with roses embroidered on the sides. Not the type of clothes I'd ever known her to wear. Her dark hair was longer now, loose, not braided. She used to braid it for her field work, every morning in the mirror down the hall while I read the newspaper, drank my coffee. I took for granted all those small perfect comforts, took for granted that she and I would be as we were then, forever and ever. And now she was alone in her new world.

Kate wavered for a moment, like she was weighing out the rest. 'She seemed upset,' she said finally. 'Hayes was walking away, and she was following him, yelling. She had a hairbrush in her hand and the whole time she was combing her hair.'

I thanked Kate; we said goodbye. It was time to be alone. For a while I wandered through the mall. It had changed so much since I'd brought Cora here as a child. There used to be fountains here, covered in beautiful white tiles flecked with gold. People threw coins in, mostly pennies, copper circles that winked underneath the water. Wishing wells. They were gone now, the fountains, the pennies. It made me think of whisky. J. P. Wiser's. You could often see their trucks around the city. When Cora was little, learning to read, she called them the wishers trucks. I hadn't thought about that in years.

Most people think of maternal instinct as tender, gentle. And it is, sometimes. But it's more than that. It's bloody, painful. It's wasps committing ovicide to benefit their own eggs. It's mother bears, full of mercy, killing their sick cubs.

———————

A month ago I went to the Queen's Way Motel near the airport, a single row of blue-painted doors along a dusty road, across from a field. *Short stays/low rates/colour television.* I saw the photo on Facebook, knew it was them. *Anybody know these two lowlifes caught 'em breaking into my car last night they stole my ...* typed beneath a photo. It showed a man in a dark sweater with a backpack already moving away from the camera, but her face was captured, just before she turned. *Yeah I see these two degenerates all the time hanging around the motel across from ...* Cora in a white jacket that didn't fit, falling off her bare shoulders, bones brittle as rock candy on a string. *Only way to deal with trash like this is you take a golf club and ...* Her eyes were almost the same but there was a blankness there I didn't recognize. *You break their jaws ...* Her eyes were like water in a glass gone cloudy. *You smash every bone in their hands. You'll never see them again.*

———————

There was no one at the front desk of the Meadows. I made my way to the stairs. Guests complained of the cold rooms, the damp carpets, the cigarette smell that wouldn't come out of the sheets. The hallways were hung with velvet paintings of ships against black skies, their sails absinthe green.

The door to Cora's room was ajar. The radio was on. She was lying on the bed, curtains drawn, lights off. *Hello, my heart.* She looked up as I stood in the doorway.

'Mom, it's you.'

I read once that's the word most said before we die: *mama, mother.* Who had recorded this? But still, I could believe it. Our first word, our last.

She was wearing an unwashed housecoat, pale cream once, but yellowed now, tied around her waist with a wide sash, and her feet were bare. Her hair was down. It had been dyed and re-dyed, a strata of dark shades. She got to her feet slowly, as if she was underwater.

I went to open the curtains.

'No, don't.' She looked ashen, her face dull grey. The housecoat dropped low over a shoulder, disclosing a shock of bone.

'Don't you miss the sunlight?'

Cora fixed her sleeve. She wrapped her arms around herself, her body lost in a slow rocking motion, soothing. 'You can get used to anything.'

But I remembered her on the frozen beach, in a pale green wool scarf, with joy in her eyes as the birds circled in the sky high above us.

On the small table was a dirty ashtray, a handful of loose coins shining like moons, a half-eaten plate of fruit, looking waxy and old and unreal, the rind red as the pairs of wax lips we used to get at Halloween.

'Where is he?'

Hayes had left, she said, an hour ago, to visit his father and ask for some money. *Don't hold your breath,* she had told him. His father had long ago cut him off. He didn't understand, she said sadly, how Hayes suffered, how sometimes the only thing that could help him was—

'Cora, it's time to come home.'

'I can't leave,' she said. She sat on the edge of the bed. Her fingers pecked at the plate of fruit, the wet, ruby pulp, picking out the seeds.

'You have nothing to read here,' I said, looking around. She'd always had something. When she didn't, she'd read the labels on jars of spices in the cupboard, tags on her dresses. I should have brought a book, a field guide to snakes, a botanical journal. I couldn't imagine Cora without anything to read.

'I can't focus very well, anyway,' she said. 'I get headaches. I'm so tired all the time.' She sat on the edge of the bed, barefoot, sucking on seeds. By her throat, like a brooch, was a bruise the size of a thumbprint.

'Do you need some money?'

Cora hesitated. 'Well, we could use it. It would make things easier. But only a little. And only if you don't mind. Hayes can't have too much money at once. It wouldn't be good.'

'Why don't you just hide it from him?' I asked, but she shook her head.

'There are no secrets between us,' she said.

I gave her five twenty-dollar bills. On the backs of the bills were poppies, scarlet amidst the maple leaf motif. She handed me back three, said any more would be too much. She thanked me. She cried a bit and said she missed me. When we went to hug goodbye, I felt the bones of her back protruding like the cold, folded stone wings of a statue.

She said, 'Come visit us again,' and I conjured up a smile, said I would, of course, and closed the door behind myself, found the stairs again. There was still no one at the front desk, but there was a tin pail out now, to catch water dripping from a crack in the ceiling, a rhythmic tick, like a clock keeping time. *Time and tide.*

I saw him before he saw me, out in the parking lot, trying the doors of cars. He had a grey sweatshirt on, the hood pulled low over his face. He was missing his beautiful watch. When he got to the gravel, where my car was parked, he looked up, his blue eyes sharp with the eyeshine of night creatures glimpsed at the edge of the woods. *Tapetum lucidum*, bright tapestry. A trait shared by predators, of creatures of the deep sea.

'Hey, Mama,' he said. 'You must have missed me.'

His dark hair, once so carefully tended, had grown wild. He wasn't wearing the cologne he'd worn before. Now he smelled like stale water, like smoke. For a moment I felt sad for him.

'Did you really think she was going to leave me?' he asked. His mouth was a ruin, nothing but a dark, gaping arch where his teeth had once been. 'She loves me now. More than you—' He coughed. 'More than you'll ever know.'

Maybe I would have walked past him then, gone to my car, but he grabbed my wrists, said, 'This time I need your help.' If he hadn't held me there like that…. 'Come on, Mama. I just need a little help. Fifty dollars. Twenty. You must have something.'

I stopped, nodded, held out my purse, slid twenty, forty, sixty dollars from it, drew out another hundred, two hundred, three hundred, until I finally lost count, all in twenties, green as new leaves. Slipped the money into his waiting hands. 'Everything I have is yours.' Maybe he said thank you, his numb lips pressed to my cheek, breathing deep. Maybe he didn't.

When I got in my car again, I looked out the window. Rain was starting to fall. The flowers would come back again now. They always do. The rain came down softly, like a mother washing the face of the earth, wiping away the old snow, the slush, making things clean. The first damp, sputtered breath of spring. *Breathe.*

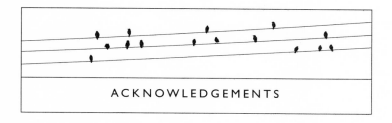

ACKNOWLEDGEMENTS

With gratitude, I want to thank everyone at Porcupine's Quill who worked to create this book, especially Stephanie Small, who edited these stories and gave them new depth and clarity. I appreciate everything you've done, all your guidance, and everything I've learned from you.

Thank you to the editors who, over the years, accepted some of these stories, which have appeared in different versions in *Hermine, Carousel, Broken Pencil, Pulp Literature, Into the Void, Lichen, sub-Terrain, The Humber Literary Review, The Impressment Gang, The Brazenhead Review* and *Apeiron Review*. I would especially like to thank S. Kennedy Sobol and *Hermine* for not only printing my story, but for helping to improve it, and Marc Laliberte and *Carousel* for being one of the first magazines to print my writing almost twenty years ago, an immeasurably encouraging experience when I was starting. I also want to thank the Ontario Arts Council for supporting through grants some of these individual stories.

I also wish to thank those in my life who have, in so many ways, been supportive and encouraging when it came not only to writing, but also to reading: my mother, Rose, who patiently wrote down my stories for me before I could write, and went with me all over the city to find Nancy Drew books; my father, Phillip, who read us everything, even the copyright pages, and is my favourite storyteller; my aunt Mary Lou DiPierdomenico, for all the words of faith, all the books you read to us, especially *Nate the Great*, and for always being there and brightening the day. I also want to thank my sisters, Grace and Sarah, for many years of listening, inspiring, and being the best sisters (and for answering all my bird questions, Sarah). With gratitude I want to thank Lindsey Bannister, always a source of support in anything big or small. I will always deeply appreciate your insight and encouragement and book recommendations. I want to acknowledge with appreciation all the years of love and support from my aunt and uncle Anne and Rocco DiPierdomenico. I wish to thank Burt and Stephanie Soulliere, for so much, but especially for every morning we went to Detroit. And finally, Jesse—I love you more than words can say, and forever.